Melting Steele

Kimberly Amato

Little Crown Media, LLC

To my father and brothers for being absolute pains in my butt my entire life. I don't think I would be as strong as I am without you.
To Felix, Joe, Mike, Jenna, Emily, & Alex for making me feel like the wealthiest aunt alive.

Contents

Foreword

Everyone deals with some kind of obsession. Some so much so, they often have issues living their daily lives. Some end up in prison for their obsession. The rest of us have the thoughts permeate our brains consistently. We sit in basements and stare at string tied from one case to another in varying colors. We try to connect the dots from things that may or may not be related. We have lives. We have the ability to intermittently turn the obsession on and off depending on the time of the day, week, or month.

We simply function within the confines of our world.

Sitting in a coffee shop, waiting for my shift to start, I can see all the obsessions oozing out of peoples' bodies. They want a large half-caf-iced-no-whip two-cups-not-too-hot, and the barista obsesses to ensure the drink is perfect so the customer comes back. Meanwhile, someone sitting behind their plethora of devices, all with the newest, name-brand chips, all on display—that person obsesses about filling their void within. It's easy to spot all of these things if you just take a moment to watch.

It's the greater loss of mankind. We hide behind these devices, these needs and desires to fill, and we effectively give in so much to our natural obsessions that we lose sight of the real world in front of us. How many people can you pass by before you look up from your phone? The person waiting for the half-caf has yet to acknowledge anyone; he's obsessed with whatever he is posting on his social media sites.

I do it all the time, but only on one topic. Maybe it's the job and the inability to see the good in mankind I used to think was there. Maybe it's the fear of what is or isn't next.

As I stand in the shower, running my hand along my scars, crying in fear, I realize . . .

I am obsessed with death.

Prologue

I've lost track of the days and months since my brother's funeral. It's like adults always say to children: time seems to fly when you grow up. I want to stop time, make it slow down and do my bidding, but it never listens. Chase still runs out the door to whatever sport he's into, Frankie walking behind him, dragging her feet, missing that last hour or two of sleep. She's getting used to being his other mother. It isn't like I gave her a choice.

I keep replaying all the events as if they will lead me to some amazing lightbulb moment. I see Officer Garrison; his attitude should have warned me. It did, but I tried to ignore it. Mistake number one. I let people take control. Mistake number two: I entrusted my family's lives into the hands of people I didn't know. Partial mistake, but still number three.

I keep thinking if I traced the phone calls to my cell through a different company, the captain wouldn't have known. Then he wouldn't have put a detail on my nephew. Then Chase would have felt more comfortable at school and with me. Maybe then I would have talked to Frankie and mended our relationship sooner. Okay, that's a stretch, because I know I was stubborn and pushing her away in my grief.

Officer James was the weak link, and my gut knew that. He was watching over Hadley, and I trusted him to protect her. Famous horror actress and her stalker fan are not a good mix, but I ignored it. When he and Garrison worked together to capture her, I went into a rage.

It was like all the years of being bullied and tormented poured out of me. The grief of watching my mother . . . my father . . . give up on life. The torture of holding my brother as he bled out while his wife lay beside him, already gone. Knowing that damn car accident could have been prevented if Officer Garrison wasn't drinking. But he was.

I killed Officer James that night. I race through the moments leading up to it, and I try to divert my actions. I keep telling myself this isn't who I am. I could never take a life. But I did. I killed the man who was trying to kill me and my friend. When he was dead, I set my sights on Garrison, and I failed that one.

I can still feel the rusty nail in my shin after falling through debris. I can hear his laugher echoing in my mind like the Joker. Then, I can feel the burn and hear the slow popping noise—loud noises and one final bang. Seeing blood pool around Garrison's head. His eyes blankly staring at nothing. The former Marine, Will, was set up to protect me. I trusted him fully. It was the only thing I did right that night.

Adults are right, though; time does slow down when you're dying. Everyone says death stalks you and can be quick, but they haven't watched a loved one die. Frankie told me it was as if the world was a meaningless wasteland. She adopted Chase when I coded on the table. It was my last wish. I wanted to die knowing he was safe. I woke up to intense pain and a long time in and out with various therapists.

You can try to reason all you like about death and how it comes to be. I've seen so much death. I've sought justice for those who have been murdered, yet there still is no real justice for my brother. There is still no justice for me.

Like I said, adults are right. Time can slow to a crawl for a short period. Obsessions, trust me—they can last a lifetime.

Chapter One

Connecting the dots was my favorite game as a kid. My mother would sit and make these long elaborate game boards on the back of envelopes. I can still see the perfectly spaced black ink dots of a specific height and width. My mother would shove a pen in my hand to play. It was a simple game, but it was our time. She always let me go first, my tongue sticking out as I pondered the best move on the completely empty board. I swear I must have imagined millions of scenarios depending on which dots connected first. Yet somehow, I always started in the bottom right corner. Maybe, after all my thoughts and conclusions, I figured it was the safest place to begin.

I think it was my safe haven. Bottom right was the one I trusted. Not because I won the game with the most completed boxes by using that strategy, but because I felt I knew what came next. I had a false sense of security, power—frankly everything. All in a little made-up game on the back of an envelope. I wish life was that simple now.

The red string lines along the wall—those are for the murders. The green ones are for money that has changed hands, but they seem to have fallen off the grid. The black, that's for my brother's case. For Garrison. For all of his moves, dealings, whatever I could find. It still baffles me how quickly the case was closed after he was killed. I was out of the hospital for a week, maybe two, when Will told me everything was sealed. It was locked away from my prying hands, but not from my friend's prying eyes. The internet is an amazing thing for those who know how to use it, but I digress.

This is my new safe haven. My basement, my strings, my case, my other life—it all sits in this basement. Leaning back in my chair, looking at the web of crime on my wall, I wonder if it is even connected at all. I have no idea. I want it to be, but I can't make a case on desire and drive. Unlike the newest crime drama on television, I have to base it on evidence and facts.

I could fabricate the whole thing. I know enough people. Unleash people online, and I'm sure in a day or so I would have enough evidence proving the mastermind behind everything. I won't though. I was raised better than that, and I won't go against my ethical code just to get vengeance. But I've thought about it. A lot. Garrison's father walks around with the air of suspicion around him, but nothing more.

I can study the strings, the moves, the motions, just like I did the dots. I want to see the best way to capture the elusive white whale. Looking at the lower right-hand corner, seeing Officer Garrison's picture, I somehow know the best place to start will always be there. His father, Irving, might be the only person in the web who's alive that I know about.

My phone vibrates on the table, pulling me out of my reverie.

"Steele."

"I'm outside; Captain sent me to get you and bring you to a crime scene."

"It's my day off."

"Chase is with my wife and kids playing games all day. Frankie's working. You're sitting in your basement hiding."

"Will, I'm working."

"On what?"

That would be the million-dollar question, wouldn't it? Do I share with him what my basement has become, or do I lie?

"I'll be out in a minute." Personally, I just ignore the situation and pray the world around me follows suit. Dropping the phone, I take one more look at my connected dots. It isn't a win by any means, but my mother never let me off easily either. Sometimes I beat her, and maybe someday I will beat this wall. Maybe.

Locking the door behind me, I reenter my world of happy moments and new beginnings. Everything negative in this world hits someone else or me indirectly. Nothing out here can hurt me anymore; at least I tell myself that. Closing the door to the house, I see Will waiting on me. Time for work.

***

The first thing I notice at this crime scene are the walls. Simple, light, khaki-colored walls. They bring life to an otherwise blank wall, but just barely. To me, they show the most death. The blood splatter is crisper on this color. The dried streaks, slightly pink, still showcase where the blood began. People always say white is better, but to me, khaki shows a hair of contrast, which helps me see the truth.

"Mr. Johnson was shot first," Victor, my trusty coroner, says from under the bed.

"His chest looks like an alien popped out of the cavity."

"I didn't eat spaghetti for months after that movie," Victor adds.

"How?"

"Considering the damage, I assume whoever did this decided to dig out the evidence."

"That takes time. No one stopped him?" Will asks quickly without thinking.

Victor slides out from under the bed and looks up at me, his expression a mix of confusion and disbelief.

"Detective, one would assume no one heard the shot or his surgical procedure."

"Mrs. Johnson is in the kitchen. The forensic team is trying to pry the cell phone out of her hand," Will mentions as he pops into the bedroom.

"They're doing what?" Victor screams as he jumps off the floor and out the room. Will watches him go, but I just smile. Victor never lets anyone touch a body before him. He gets very jealous in a green-eyed monster kind of way. He swears it's due to his desire to have things done well the first time. Personally, I think he loves being the person to find the evidence that may or may not break a case. I know I would.

Reaching over to the end table, I grab Mr. Johnson's wallet and open it. Credit cards and cash are all here. Placing it back down, I notice an identification badge. Mr. Johnson smiles in the photo, but it's the name of the company that gets my attention: Garrison Developments. This man worked for Irving Garrison, and my heart begins to race. Turning to see Will standing there, concern on his face. I hold up the badge, and he immediately understands.

"How does it look down there?" I mutter, trying to slow the racing of my heart.

"Not good." Will looks around the room. "It gets worse."

"How does it get worse? Two victims, one shot while he was sleeping. His wife was murdered in the kitchen trying to call for help. I think that's pretty bad as is."

"Son was found in the closet."

My heart stops in my chest, my breath hitches, and I feel sick. You can show me bodies all day, floaters, whatever, but I have never been able to handle when horrible things have been done to kids. I might not have faith in humanity, but I will never understand hurting a child.

Walking down the hall, the big letters spelling DANNY stand out on the stark white door. Using my left latex-gloved hand, I push the door open. Action figures litter the floor, the bed is unmade, clothes sit folded on the dresser, and a book bag rests by the door. Everything looks as it should for a young boy's room—except for the bloody red prints on the floor leading to the closet. I'd say they were shoe prints, but it looks like something was over the treads to prevent markings. Basically, they are smudges useless to any investigation.

Slowly, one covered shoe in front of the other, I make my way to the closet. I take a deep breath, trying to prepare myself for the carnage my eyes will dissect in a few steps. Pulling the door open, my eyes see a small boy of about nine, lying on his side, a Mickey Mouse doll in his arms and a peaceful expression on his face. His lips are blue, along with his fingers.

"You didn't touch him?"

"Saw the stains on the floor; figured Victor would want to look at him first."

Leaning down, I get a better look at what might be his fatal injury. No gunshot wound. No handprints on the front of his neck. It looks like he just went to sleep in the closet. Using my small flashlight, I highlight his neck, and that's when I see the bruising toward the back. His neck was snapped. Quick, simple, and some say it's painless. Nothing is ever fully painless; death sure as hell isn't. Turning off my light, I stand up and try to center myself. There's this rage that builds up deep inside me when kids are hurt. Maybe it's because I have Chase. Maybe it's because the majority of kids are innocent. Maybe it's because I can't handle it. Either way, I am going to hate this fucking case.

Backing out of the scene and into the hallway, I lean against the wall and let out the breath I was holding in for what felt like an eternity.

"Clean?"

"Snapped his neck. I don't know whether to say it was kind or cruel. Probably placed him where he found him."

"Still killed him." Will was right. Regardless of the procedure of death, the end result was this murderer wiped out a light before the flame was fully lit.

"So, the killer shot Dad but not the boy?"

"Why?"

"Won't know until Victor gives us more information to work with."

I look from him to the other side of the hallway wall. Realization hits me like a ton of bricks. My day is about to become a nightmare, and there is nothing I can do about it.

"Get Udall on the phone."

Will looks at me quizzically as I reach forward and pull a family photo off the wall. I show Will the photo, and his eyes widen in surprise.

"How the hell did we miss that?"

"Because we were off today and the B team came in?"

"That's not an excuse." Will pulls out his phone and clicks a name in his contact book. "They can figure out the victims' names but don't fucking look to see if the daughter is missing? That's called basic officer training 101."

"Either way, we need to find out if the kid is missing or just at a friend's house."

Someone picks up the other line, and I can hear Will's voice running a mile a minute. He's not happy, and neither am I. This was a big mistake, and someone should lose their job over it. If she's at a friend's house,

great. We should have had her at the precinct with child services assist-
ing. Instead, we are now battling time and a whole new set of crap.

I can feel the scapegoat conversation coming when we hit the office.
My sense of sound seems to fade away as I walk down the hall. My eyes
dart around, taking in everything. The door opens, and the image of a
young girl comes into view. Posters on the wall of some band I know
nothing about. Pictures on a corkboard of friends laughing in unison. Her
name, Kaley, plastered on anything with glitter glue. Everything is neat,
untouched, and calm, like she wasn't even here. Either she wasn't here,
or she was the target.

Looking around the room, nothing seems out of place, but it doesn't
feel right either. Chase's room is a perpetual mess. Hell, my room is a
mess. If not for Frankie, I doubt I would know what color my carpet is.
My gut is screaming at me; this isn't right.

"Captain wants us back at the station. Victor is handling everything
here and says he'll call us when he has something."

"Make him get the techs to go over every inch of this room."

"He told me to tell you, 'I was planning on it.' Don't kill the messenger,"
Will says like a robot reading the movie times.

Leave it to Victor's cockiness to give me some hope for a lead in this
case. I try to be an optimist. I have good moments too, but my gut is
a pessimist by trade. It's rarely wrong. I know we're already against the
clock, and whatever she was wanted for, she's already gone, either dead
or worse. I prefer not to think about the worse ideas. Truthfully, death
is a nicer outcome than what I can envision. Call it intuition or just plain
pessimism. One way or another, Kaley will never be found alive.

***

Seeing officers running from one end of the room to the other, random
papers in their hands, proves to me they are in what I like to call police
panic mode. It's not a true panic mode really, but there isn't another way
to describe the rushed movement, the hurried conversations, and the
overall hyper energy of the place. My steps are slower, more deliberate as
I follow a fast-moving former Marine to the captain's office. Sliding calmly
into the chair, I watch the two men talk animatedly. It's very interesting
watching them interact. Behavior can tell you so much about the conversation. The captain's hand keeps waving about as if it's making some
more of an impact to the conversation. Will's arms folded defensively
across his chest tell me the conversation is not going well. No wonder I
always think Italians are fighting when they talk; their hands never stop
moving.

"Detective Steele!" Shaking the fog from my brain, I look up to see both Will and Tyler staring at me in an unhappy way.

"Yes."

"Do you have anything you want to add to this conversation?"

"What do you want me to add? We have three bodies. The father worked for Garrison Developments, which may or may not have anything to do with his death."

"First, you stay out of that rabbit hole. Second, maybe you can explain why the hell we didn't notice a little girl was missing!"

"We weren't there at the time the house was cleared."

Tyler walks around his desk and slams his door for effect. Sitting down on the edge of his desk, he slowly rubs his eyes with frustration. Will slumps into the chair next to me, unsure of what to do.

"Captain, we weren't even supposed to be there. You requested we go there, and we did. I'm not pointing fingers or blaming anyone. The most important part is figuring out where Kaley is, who took her, and praying we can get her back."

"Officers are calling anyone in the home phone's memory as well as the mother's and father's cell phones. If she is at a friend's house—or anywhere else for that matter—we will find her. In the meantime, we are investigating the murders," Will says calmly for the first time since we learned of the missing young girl.

"Okay." The captain stands up and stretches his neck. "I want the two of you on this."

"We've got a department to handle that; we need to focus on the three homicides, sir," Will pipes up from the comfort of his chair.

"This was a massive fuck-up by our division, so forgive me if I expect my two best to actually focus on more than one thing."

The captain sits back down in his chair and silence falls over the room. In all the rush to get a task force looking for the girl, something notoriously gets overlooked.

"Why didn't she call the police?"

Will looks at me quizzically. "Kaley?"

"Yeah, if she was the target, why didn't she call the police?"

"Maybe she wasn't home?"

"Or he already had her and needed to remove the family?"

The captain picks up his phone and punches a few buttons. "Get me a trace on Kaley Johnson's phone. I want to know where it was for every second of yesterday. I want a list of calls, texts . . . anything and everything. Dump it all." He slams his phone down.

My phone rings and I look at the caller ID; it's Frankie. I push the side button, cutting off the new ringtone of Frankie and Chase telling me to answer the phone. It's a constant reminder of the love I have with this great family. Plus, it's an improvement over my old one of just Chase telling me to answer the phone. At least now that he's a bit older, I can understand him. Well, mostly anyway.

The captain looks at me, but I can't tell if he's annoyed or just frustrated by the situation we find ourselves in.

"I'll have the techs comb through everything. Hopefully, something pops up from the last twenty-four hours."

"Will and I will ask around, look at school friends. The usual. See if anything comes up."

"Victor have anything?"

I open my mouth to speak as my phone comes to life once again. Disconnecting the call, I say, "Not that I know of. I'm waiting on him to call." The captain stares at me with the eyes of a parent admonishing their children. "But why don't we just head on down there and see what's new."

"That would be a great idea. And, Jasmine, you stay away from Garrison."

"Sir, I follow the evidence."

"If it leads there, Detective Everts will handle it. I don't need your name attached to another member of that family. We don't have a vendetta, understand?"

Without saying another word, I stand up and walk out of the captain's office. My instinct tells me that the job might have nothing to do with the murders. Doesn't mean I don't want to ram down the door, guns blazing, and demand answers. I don't have a vendetta against the man who killed my brother and his wife in a DWI. Nor do I have a grudge against the man who put bullets in me before Will took him down. I do not have anything against his father and everyone else that might be involved. Not at all. As a detective, I have a mission to ensure justice is served, and I plan on finishing it.

It's still an odd thing to me, walking down the stairs into the morgue—the big, empty window looking through to another world, one we will all see, eventually. Yet, when you're on this side of the glass, that place seems so far away. I'm abnormal though. I've been on both sides of the glass. I remember Victor made me stand out here when he looked over my brother and his wife. Lifting my hand and placing it against the divider, I can still feel the emotions coursing through my veins that day, but they are calmer now.

I can feel Will watching me closely as he walks into the room looking for Victor. He's learned when to bother me and when to let me be with my memories. When my father died, I never stepped foot in the morgue. I didn't want to see him like that. When my mother died, Victor emptied the entire floor. I sat in his chair, holding her hand, talking to her as if she would sit up and give me a hug. It's an odd thing for a daughter to lose her mother, her best friend, her confidant. Sure, we move on, make friends, and get married, but no one will ever come close to our mommy.

Will pops his head out of the door and looks at me. "Just thinking," I mumble to him. He walks over and stands next to me, his arms folded, his demeanor cold.

"There's an odd divide here. Life on one side of the door, death on the other. I didn't get that over there."

"It's a strange sense of comfort, being separated. Kind of like, 'hey it's steak, with no thought to where it comes from.'" I nervously let the words tumble out of my mouth. He chuckles a little, but I continue to stare at the white sheet-covered bodies.

"Yeah, sometimes I wish we had that. One minute you're talking to your buddy and the next minute he's on the floor. All you can think of"—he takes a deep breath and exhales slowly—"all I could think of was where the hell the sniper was hiding. My friend was dead a few feet away from me, and I couldn't do a thing for him."

The conversation hangs, waiting for one of us to pick it up and continue. Yet, neither of us do. We stand next to one another, staring at the room of death, waiting.

"You know they aren't going anywhere. So, if you'd like to stop standing guard and come in, I would love to share with you the vast amount of nothing I found," Victor says as he strolls past us, peanut butter sandwich in hand.

"Didn't they fine you for eating down here?"

"My dear Jasmine, they don't fine the master. They give him a slap on the wrist and avert their eyes."

"I'd avert my eyes too. That smells horrible," Will says as he waves his hands in front of his face.

"I assure you my organic peanut butter isn't what you're smelling." Victor casually walks over to a body and pulls back the sheet, revealing the mother. "She had egg on her face, literally. Quite smelly stuff if left out long enough."

"That help give you time of death?"

"No, but she was in full rigor, ergo why your maniacs with hacksaws were trying to pry the cell phone out of her hand."

"How long are we talking, Victor?"

Victor covers the mother back up and walks back to his desk. "I'd estimate they've all been dead for about twelve hours."

I look over at Will and nod my head. The captain needs to know that our timeline has not only changed, it's pretty much disappeared.

"Expand the search and dump the mom's phone. On it." He rushes out of the morgue, bypasses the elevator, and heads up the stairs.

"I'm sorry." Victor looks at me, a guilty, childlike expression on his face.

"Not your fault."

"No, but I hate being the bearer of bad news."

"Vic, you think I ever come down here expecting some chipper encounter? You cut up dead people. No matter which way you look at it, you always see people on their worst day. Hell, one day you might still be doing this and cut my body up."

"Been there, done that." His words silence me. "I'll quit before I have to do that again." Watching him slowly eat his sandwich, almost mechanically as he tries to clear the thoughts from his mind, I wish I knew what to say to help him, but the words fail me. I was dead. He saved my life. Thank you doesn't seem to cut it.

"They have a daughter." Victor's attention turns back to me quickly.

"That explains the mad rush upstairs." I simply nod in response. "You think she's gone."

"My gut tells me this was a professional. He meticulously kills Margaret Johnson first in the kitchen, slices her throat from left to right at an upward angle. Very close and intimate."

"So, a right-handed killer who is taller than the wife at . . ."

"She is approximately five feet seven inches."

"So, a right-handed average-height male; narrows it down. Next?"

"Daniel Johnson, cervical fracture due to massive torque applied to his neck. Based on the bruising patterns, I would guess it was another left-to-right movement. Considering Mrs. Johnson's injuries, it would appear accurate."

"Okay, so he goes into the kitchen, kills the wife while she's making dinner. Goes up the stairs, kills the boy."

"Then he kills Lester Johnson. This is where it gets very complicated, so just shut up and listen before commenting."

He stares at me, and I concede by nodding in response.

"He was shot, but it appears the bullet nicked an artery, causing him to bleed internally. Based on the tissue, I can only guess that a knife was used repeatedly to speed up the process."

"Okay, so the bullet missed its mark, and the perp finished the job with a knife. What's complicated in that scenario?"

"The bullet was meant to fail."

"Okay, now you lost me."

"The bullet disintegrated when it entered his abdomen. Based on the evidence left, frangible ammo was used to incapacitate Mr. Johnson before more final blows could be administered."

"He wanted it to be personal."

"Based on the evidence I found, my gut tells me Daddy was made out to be an example."

"Of?"

"I don't know, but whoever did this wanted his death to be gruesome." Taking a few steps over to the freezer wall, my hand grazes number twenty-three. "You keep your word?"

"If I have to, yes. Frankie made it clear, lucky number and all for the afterlife. You're awfully morbid, you know? Maybe take Frankie out on a date? You know . . . the woman who happens to be your longtime girlfriend that you should marry already? Or skip the proposal and just have a fun night?"

"I'm not morbid. I prepare for the horrific and enjoy the normal. And I do take Frankie out, but we're taking it slow. She's been dealing with Hadley and trying to get her back into auditioning."

"Can't blame the poor girl after what she went through. You might have been shot, but she was there too, Jasmine. She was threatened, and she watched you die from your injuries. She's afraid and dealing with heavy PTSD from it."

"She needs to get back into auditioning again, use the publicity for her acting career. She has to make a living too."

"She's doing the convention circuit. Although, you and I both know that isn't much safer, but she feels it is. You could just call her and say hi. That might go a long way in helping her recover." I hear Frankie's and Chase's voice scream from my cell phone. Hitting the side button, I cut it off.

"You told me she's okay, so we're good. I'm going to head out. Call me if you find anything else." Turning my back to Victor, I head for the elevator.

"She doesn't blame you, even if you feel responsible. Just call her, Jasmine." I know Victor means business when he calls me Jasmine. Like my mother calling me out on my crap. The difference is, I listened to her. My friends who I consider family, sometimes. Not now though.

Hearing the elevator ding its arrival, I enter the box and push my floor. He stares at me as if imploring me to say something. Once again, words fail me, and I simply let the doors close.

Getting out of the elevator on the twentieth floor, I make a right and head down a hallway I know very well. My mind is full of tangential thoughts as people smile at me on the way. Simple nodding in response, the memory of my mother informing me a nod and a smirk were impolite rushes across my memory. It's always interesting to me how our brains remember things and when it decides to make itself known. Opening the door to the last office on the right, I see the chair behind the desk sits empty. Closing the door behind me, I walk inside and lie down on the leather couch. I swear I could fall asleep in the safe arms of this worn thing. My eyes, heavy with thought, close of their own accord.

"Contrary to popular opinion, most people prefer the chairs. You missed lunch and didn't answer my calls, so I assume you caught a case. Either that or we have something more serious to talk about," Frankie lightheartedly says as I hear her close the door. So many words fight for dominance to exit my mouth first, but the logjam causes a low, nonsensical sound to exit my mouth. I hear her walk toward me, her steps making a distinct sound as she drags her heels on the carpet. The leather chair sighs as she sits across from me.

"You want to tell me what's on your mind? Is it the case or something else?"

"Logjam." I can hear her chuckle just a bit at my reference. She's been here before.

"Pick one thing and just say it," she quietly suggests. As if it were that simple. As if I could stick my hand into my brain and just pull out one idea, somehow manage to force my mouth to understand the process and speak. Opening my eyes, I look sideways at her, my 'You have to be shitting me' look. She simply leans back in the chair, and I see the psychologist in her is about to take over.

"Don't give me that look. You know damn well it is that simple. Just focus on one thing, take a breath, and say it. If a schizophrenic off his meds can learn to do it, I'm sure you—with no ailments whatsoever—can as well."

Looking up at the ceiling, I take a deep breath and exhale slowly to waste time. "How is Hadley doing? And I don't mean she's doing as well as can be expected, I mean from the shrink side of you, how is she doing?"

"You know I can't and won't discuss that with you. Suffice it to say she's doing okay given the circumstances."

"Frankie, I'm serious."

"If it were that important to you, you would have picked up the phone and called her. Yet here you are on my couch, grilling me about our friend. I know you're having a difficult time dealing with what happened."

I give her my sideways glance again. She simply holds her hand up to stop my attempt to argue.

"No, I'm not a fool. I live with you. I know you come to bed after me and wake up before our alarm. You spend hours in that locked dungeon of yours, but I haven't pressed the issue. Not because it isn't an issue, but because I've learned a long time ago to let you talk when you're ready. You both went through hell, but the rest of us did as well, and frankly, Vincent and I are not going to give either of you information on the other.

This is not kindergarten or spy versus spy; you're both adults, so pick up the damn phone."

Swinging my legs to the floor, I run my hands through my hair before rubbing my eyes. Anything to give my mind a moment to catch up to the verbal lashing I just got.

"It's not that simple."

"Jazz, we've been down this road, and you looked like a pin cushion at the end of it. I'm not saying you have to face everything that happened, but saying 'hello' and 'how are you' is not that difficult. Stop hiding behind your guilt and be an adult."

"This how you talk to your patients?" I try to defuse the situation with some sarcasm. She stares at me, her eyes set, arms across her middle, body language speaking to my lack of respect. My mother would have smacked the back of my head or, worse, taken away my coffee for my horrible idea, but Frankie just looks all boss like. No wait, more like a teacher when you are caught cheating off the kid next to you. When in doubt, you change the subject or blame the person you were cheating off of.

"What kind of person kills two people with planned precision, shows mercy when killing a child, but takes another as a prisoner?" She shakes her head, rubs her eyes, but I can see she's accepting my change of topic. It's what she does because she knows me or loves me or just tolerates me. The action speaks volumes to me, regardless of the reason. She lets me be as long as I understand I eventually have to talk. It's the whole compromise thing we work on a lot.

"You want a professional or personal answer to that?"

"Whatever you've got."

"A sick fuck." We both break out laughing at her sharp, no-holds-barred answer.

"Beyond that," I calm down and ask her. She stands, walks toward the window. and looks out at the city lights.

"Depends on a lot of things." She crosses her arms, and the slight hint of crow's feet at the corners of her eyes tells me the gears in her brain are spinning fast.

"Such as?"

"Manner of death. Time. Evidence."

"One GSW slash stabbing, one snapped neck, one sliced throat. Victor's working on locking down a timeframe. Minimal at best."

"That's not a lot to go on."

"It's all I've got at the moment."

I watch as she inhales and exhales slowly a few times. It's something she started doing when I was in the hospital. Maybe to center herself or her thoughts. Sometimes though, you know it's to block her emotions from coming to the forefront. No matter how many times we talk, fight, or do the normal things couples do, there are times when I find her watching me. She'll just breathe like that for a few seconds, stare at me intently, and walk away. The scraping of her heels against the carpet brings my focus back to Frankie, her pacing slow, deliberate. Each pace with her right hand swinging ever so slightly, as if she's figuring out a difficult *New York Times* crossword. Who are we kidding? They dumbed that shit down years ago. Trust me, I can easily finish them now.

"He obviously had a plan."

"Okay."

"I know that seems obvious, but it's important."

"I know, but in this case how is the plan more important than normal?"

"The girl was the target. He systematically killed the mother, then the son, and then the father before taking the daughter." Frankie stops her pacing and turns to face me. "Was she home during the attack?"

"Right now we're not sure. Dumping phones and scouring over everything we have on the Johnson family. If we're lucky, Kaley's phone is still on and we can find her."

"What?"

"I know it's the stupid wishful thinking of an optimistic fool."

"You're a perpetual pessimist, so no, but you said Kaley Johnson?"

"Yeah, why?"

"I need to see a warrant."

I stand and walk to Frankie, somewhat lost as to her comment. She stands with her arms across her chest in a defiant stance, but her eyes are pleading for help. Behavior can be such an improper science or just a clusterfuck as my brother said.

"Why would I need a warrant?"

Frankie walks behind her desk and places her fingertips on the solid wood. She pushes a button on her phone, and a voice echoes through the speaker. "Yes, Doc?"

"Brian, can you please come in here?"

"Why do you need Brian, your muscle, to come in here? Frankie, what the hell is going on?"

The door opens, and a six-foot muscle man in a tiny suit walks in the door and looks at me. His confusion mirrors mine as he looks back and forth between the two of us.

"Doc?"

"Brian, can you please show the detective out?"

"No, Brian, you're not touching me until someone tells me what the hell is going on."

"I told you, detective, I need to see a warrant before discussing a patient. It's almost four in the evening. I suggest you get moving."

Brian walks up to me and gently places his hand on my back.

"Detective, please?"

"Anyone tell you your suit's too tight?"

He just smiles at me as I feel him push me toward the door. Giving Frankie a glance over my shoulder, I see her looking down at her desk. Part of me understands her professionalism, but dammit, warn a girl next time before flipping the bitch switch.

***

Walking across the grass field, I'm late. The lacrosse game has to be in the fourth quarter, which means I am rather angry at myself. Seeing Frankie sitting at the row's end on the bleachers cheering is a beautiful sight. Yet, I still want to yell about our conversation a few hours ago. She could have just told me the truth about Kaley instead of all the pomp and circumstance. She has a lot of explaining to do. I stand next to the bleachers and wait for her to start the conversation. Looking across the field, I see Chase—number five—running down the field toward the opposite goal. He takes a shot from a pretty decent distance, and Frankie jumps up with her hopes high, only to sigh when the goalie stops it. Slowly, she lowers herself back to the bench.

"You can come up here, you know," she says without looking at me.

"I could, but the game's almost over."

"I told him where you were."

"I figured."

"He's not upset."

"I am." Those two words grab her attention, and she turns to face me.

"I freelance with the police department. I had to keep everything aboveboard. I did to you what I would have done to anyone else coming into my office asking questions about a patient."

"You could have just been direct and told me she was a patient."

"That's never worked on you and you know it." She turns her attention back to the game.

"I have your warrant."

"I never doubted that."

"How's he doing?"

"One goal, which will irritate him, but he is great on defense. Just like someone else I know."

"That was one time." I laugh as I watch Chase running after an errant pass.

"Which is why you are no longer allowed to play in the annual basketball game anymore."

"What can I say? I'm competitive."

She says nothing as the two of us watch Chase get knocked over by a bigger kid. Frankie jumps to her feet and screams at the referee. Chase shakes it off and runs back to the play. He turns to see Frankie standing and screaming. He'll reprimand her for that later. My first instinct used to be to jump, but after one baseball game, he asked me to please stop. Granted, those were not any of the words he used, but I got the point. He loves me enough to politely let me down. Of course, that was when we would train together. Basketball, baseball, hockey—I could play it all. It was bonding time. Now he plays this game I never understood. He has practice after school and on weekends without me. It's a bitter pill to swallow, losing that connection. I guess that is why my mom always insisted on going to the park with me. Even in high school, she'd help me sharpen my skills with a game of catch, fielding, or batting practice. When I blew my knee out, that ended, and with it our bonding time. I wonder if this is her way of cursing me. Chase might be my brother's son, but she did wish I'd have a kid just like me. Now I do. I am so screwed.

"Aunt Jazz, what was Aunt Frankie screaming about? It was a clean hit." My attention is brought back by the youngster standing in front of me. Turning around, I see Frankie a few steps ahead carrying his bag.

"She's just protective of you."

"Like you were?" He wraps his arm around my waist, and we head toward the car.

"Still am, little man. Just not as verbal about it."

"Much appreciated. You were late."

"Yeah, had to see a judge."

"Don't the lawyers do that?"

"Yup, but this lawyer insisted I come with."

"Sounds like fun," he says ironically. He looks up at me and smiles. He's getting to the age where I am unsure if those are innocent or mischievous looks anymore. Either way, he's more like my brother every waking moment. Just as quickly as his smile comes, it disappears as he turns and runs to catch up with Frankie. He jumps and knocks her hat off her head before running ahead of her. She drops his bag and takes off in a sprint. Watching the two of them brings meaning to my life. These moments of pure joy uninhibited by death or the surrounding negative . . . they are perfect.

"Aunt Jazz, first one home gets to control the remote!" he says as the car engine roars to life. Picking up his bag, I know there is no way I can win this race. Besides, he hasn't caught on that we like the same shows yet. I'll let him think he has control. Eventually he'll learn knowledge is power. Until then, I'll let him be a kid.

Chapter Two

The flickering sound of a fluorescent light permeates my dreams. My eyes slowly open, fighting the light as it blinds me. My hands, unmoving, are tied to something. My legs, numb. Mouth gagged. This can't be real.

"Wakey, wakey!" I hear as cold water slams against my face, instantly sobering me up from my half sleep. Spitting out and blinking away the water, I take in my surroundings. The concrete walls are crumbling around me. The crunch of gravel under someone's boots sounds just out of my line of vision.

"See, this is how I told you it would end."

Lifting my head, I look down at my legs; blood pours from my right one from a rusty nail wound. I don't feel it, but my mind registers that I should feel pain, so I do. It's excruciating. Screaming into my gag, I feel the skin under my wrists and ankles chafe and split with every jerk of my limbs. Everything in me tells me to stay calm, but nothing in my body is listening. I was trained to manage my emotions. Keep them at bay. Have a steady hand, aim, but don't fire unless you must. If you must, never miss. All while having absolute control.

As I feel my body twitching, fighting, twisting against my restraints, my mind soars, trying to fight the impulses, but memories begin flashing through it and all hope is lost. Fear is reigning over me, and there is nothing I can do.

"Now, now, fighting never helped. Look what happened to me?"

Garrison walks into the light, blood trickling down between his eyes, his smile as bright and bold as ever. My body stops shaking and my eyes stay on him.

"If you had just let things go, had let me handle the case, none of this would have happened." He walks closer, the edge of a hunting knife catching my eye. He notices.

"It was my father's. He used to take me hunting all the time as a kid, but you know that already. It's in my file." He slides the blade up my right leg, pausing at my open wound. Looking up at me, he smiles viciously, and I try to voice my pleas through the gag. As he tips the knife up, I watch it enter my skin slowly. Once again, my brain lets me feel the pain in my legs, and I scream until I'm out of breath. As he pulls out the knife, the blood on the blade is black as night. He looks at it, pleased.

"You and I aren't very different. You read my file; you know how fucked up I am. Hell, I killed your brother and his wife for a few shots of Patron and a couple of beers. That is how much their lives meant to me, but you . . ." He slowly turns and his eyes lock with mine. "You're doing this all on your own. Just like I did."

He leans over my body, so close I can smell the stale cigarettes on his breath. As he places the knife above my heart, I feel it slightly breaking my skin.

"Maybe I should have let you live and watch it take you over, eat you alive. This shouldn't hurt, but it will."

He slams the blade into my chest, and it feels like my heart is exploding like a water-filled balloon. Shaking violently, he holds my head and sings a lullaby to calm me.

***

Shooting up in bed, my hand frantically runs over my chest on its own accord. These dreams are coming more frequently now. Every one of them is the same as the last. Each time the pain feels more real, no matter how much I try to deny it. Rubbing my chest, I feel as if I've been stabbed. I swear it takes several breaths and my eyes darting around the room before my heart stops slamming in my chest. Looking over to Frankie, I see she's still sleeping. That's a first.

Slipping out from under the covers as quietly as possible, I slink out of the bedroom and close the door behind me. Mindlessly following the low light at the end of the hall, I see Chase sitting up in bed with his game controller in his hand.

"You're supposed to be sleeping." My voice causes him to jump and almost fall out of bed. Normally I would laugh, but not after that nightmare.

"I should say the same thing to you, Aunt Jazz," he whispers as he finds his controller, pausing his game.

"Online?"

"No, just leveling up."

"You have school in the morning so turn it off, okay?" I turn to leave him alone.

"You're not gonna tell Aunt Frankie, are you?" The childlike innocence comes back in his voice, and I turn back around, shaking my head. He knows she would remove that system in a heartbeat, unlike myself, who has a system in the basement so he and I can play online together. The days of him sitting on my lap while we played the newest Lego game are long gone. He also knows how to play me like a cheap fiddle. Frankie disciplines better than I can when he looks at me with those big eyes of his.

"No, buddy, you're fine." He looks at me as if I'm some math equation he's trying to decipher. If Aunt Jazz answers a question talking five miles per hour and Aunt Frankie is snoring at three miles per hour, how long does it take you to become annoyed with stupid, improbable questions? The question makes me smile, internally at least.

"You remember when I first moved in with you?"

"How could I forget?"

"You let me sleep with you to make the monsters go away. You always said the bed was too big anyway."

"Well, who knew there were so many hiding in your room? Had I known, I would have had Hadley come in and sage the place or something." I try to lighten the conversation, even though my body still feels the pain of my dream.

"Nah, that would have made my room smell horrible." He smiles brightly at me.

"Goodnight, buddy."

"My bed is too big." It's a simple phrase, but it makes my heart melt. I want to walk into his room and climb into bed with him, make the monsters go away, but I can't. This isn't a battle he needs to win, nor should he have to deal with it. This is mine and mine alone. Not trusting my voice, I just smile at him and close the door behind me.

✳✳✳

Passing through my game room area, I find the hidden key and open the door to my dungeon. The plush carpet turns to cold tile under my feet. The walls are littered with memories, dead ends, and stunted dreams. I wish I could make sense of it all, but sometimes the mind is so overcome with information we can barely process it. Just like with our cell phones, hiding behind the mask of technology so we almost always miss what is right in front of our faces. I feel that way now. This history, these strings, clippings, and images are all in front of my face, yet I see nothing. It is where I hide.

Sitting down in my chair, it is easy to get lost in the mass of information. Strings from case to case, image to image. Red, green, and black string. Simple colors with such meaning behind them simply by what they connect. Looking at the photo directly above my desk, my hand wanders to rub my chest again, my mind making me feel pain long gone, yet still in my memory.

Victor stands above my worn-out and tired body, his hands covered in my blood, his mouth open, screaming orders. It's from the hospital when the crime photographer thought I would die. He chose to document as much as possible. It's such a weird thing to see all of that blood come out of your body and not remember any of it.

"Keep it simple, stupid," I mumble to myself. I have a tendency to overlook things and miss what is directly in front of me. Sure, there is always a bigger picture, but we can be so overwhelmed by how big it really is that we can't see the tree for the forest. At least my mother always said that.

She also called you her peanut when you towered over her by seven inches. I laugh to myself. I know what she meant, but it still makes me smile every time I think about it. It was better than when she would scream "tall person" or, better yet, "moose." No idea how that nickname came about, but once again, I digress.

If she were alive, what would she do? How would she handle this? I wonder that sometimes. Maybe because I find solace in the idea of her still being here as a guide who I could trust. Looking over the photos of the hospital stay, I know that would have killed her had she not been dead already. She never had to deal with my brother dying. If she lived through that and then my brush with death, I doubt she would leave me alone. What is it called? Helicopter parenting. She would have hovered over me, making sure I was okay. Of course, it would have been in support, but also because of her fear. I'm the only girl on both sides of the family. In addition to that that, I'm her baby girl.

"A son's your son until he takes a wife, a daughter's your daughter for the rest of your life," I say, once again mumbling the line I know by heart.

"I wish you were here to make this go away. Maybe make the dots clearer, my mind calmer. I want to climb into your leather chair like when I was a kid and smell your perfume." A lone tear falls from my right eye, and I quickly wipe it away. I am an adult; I have said goodbye. I wish this hole would go away.

"But it doesn't, does it? It never goes away, just changes in size or dominance. You told me that when Grandma died. You said your heart was broken, but life heals it. We healed it for you. Watching your children live, having children fulfill their dreams, and you never once complained about being left behind." Opening the top desk drawer on my right, I pull out an old photo of my mother holding me in full catcher's gear, a huge trophy in one hand, the other wrapped around her neck. The colors are faded and worn from being handled so much. I could scan it and restore it, but it wouldn't feel the same.

"Frankie says talking helps, but when you can't answer, it hurts, you know? There are so many things I want to ask you about dealing with Chase. What do I do when he hits high school? How do I give him the sex talk? What do I do when he answers me back? Well, okay, I know what to do with that last one. I just send him to Frankie." I laugh at my comment.

"It's funny how much I grew up and became this big detective with a tough exterior, but I still want my mommy." Placing the picture back into the drawer, I close it, the sound harsh and final.

Looking back up at the board, I stand and take the black string in between my fingers, following it from point to point, stopping at a family photo. Garrison stands proudly in his uniform after graduating from the police academy. His father Irving and his mother Patricia wrap their arms around his shoulders. A clipping next to the photo reads, "Real estate developer's wife dies in apparent suicide." He's lost everything, with only his company and connections to hold him up at night. He's not the head; I know that. His money was new; no schooling, not smart enough or powerful enough to make the moves in city hall. He's a player on the chess board, and unbeknownst to them . . . it's my turn to move.

Chapter Three

Sitting in the kitchen waiting for the coffee to finish, I hear Chase up and about, his footsteps rushing from the bedroom to the bathroom in the hall and back again. I assume he set his alarm, but after hours of gaming at night, I doubt getting up was simple. I guess I do discipline by letting him suffer through the consequences of his actions. I wish other parents did the same, but like them, I would bail Chase out of major drama in the blink of an eye.

"Please tell me there's coffee." Frankie drags herself into the kitchen, her eyes still at half-mast, her sandy-blonde hair looking like it was in a wind tunnel, all knotted and pointing in all directions.

"Of course," I reply and take a sip of the delicious lifeline. "Chase make it?"

Footsteps slam on the floor above us, with various mumblings about being late.

"Nope."

"Was he up all night playing that shooting game?" She sits next to me, and I raise an eyebrow at her.

"Oh, don't think I don't know about you two and your midnight game fest."

"I thought you were sleeping."

"Yes, well a woman always knows." She laughs a little at her own comment, her hazel eyes brightening with her smile. "Besides, I know when you're not in bed."

"Oh yeah? How is that?"

"The fact that you don't roll me over when I snore and that I have covers?"

"I do not steal the covers; you kick them off."

"Yes, I do, but that's usually when you have the heat on inferno."

"Not my fault you're always hot."

"I'm hot, huh?" Shaking my head, I lean forward and give her a kiss.

"Seriously? That is so gross guys!" Laughing, I turn to see Chase standing in the doorway, looking the worse for wear.

"Bus will be here soon."

"But I can't find my phone."

"Maybe you should have gone to bed on time and woken up at a decent hour to find it." Frankie leans back in her chair, a smug look on her face. "Or you could have just put it by the charging cable in your room. Oh wait, you lost that last week."

"You are so not being fair, Aunt Frankie," he says with the most adorable pout on his face.

"Yes, well when you pay for the cables, the phone, or the bill, you can argue with me."

The bus horn honk outside. Chase looks mortified as he rushes out the door, mumbling something about hating us. It's the age.

"He hates us again," I mutter as I continue to indulge in my coffee.

"Yep, until he's thirty he probably will." She leans forward at the table, her hands wrapped around her mug. She's got her serious, thoughtful look, or the coffee is wrecking her stomach. I can't tell the difference sometimes.

"Ever think what he would be like if we were the only ones who raised him?"

"Frankie, I doubt Chase has a comparison chart in his bedroom with pros and cons of being punished by me or my brother."

"I mean if he was always ours." She looks into her coffee and realization hits me. Right now would be a perfect time to create that black hole in Sweden or something to swallow the world up. Or just do it below me and watch me swim.

"You going to say something?"

"What's there to say?"

"I'm a psychologist; there's always something to say." She looks up at me, her smile not reaching her eyes. They reflect my fear mixed with her own.

"We're both too old."

"You're thirty and I'm thirty-two. I don't think that's too old, but that isn't the only way."

"Maybe not, but are we stable enough financially, emotionally, whatever-ally to handle another child, let alone a baby? Not to mention the fact that we are not a traditional household. They might have some stupid rule that says we can't adopt or have a kid because we're together. Maybe they won't like us because we're not married and living in sin . . . even though according to other people, we're sinning by . . . well . . . being us."

"I wouldn't object to an older child, maybe a toddler? I just think Chase would be a great big brother. Maybe it would do him some good to have a brother or sister around. Not to mention we're in a good place now. If you look at money, we'll never have another child. Trust me, no one is ever financially ready, or they wouldn't be on my couch with stress coming out of their ears." She stops and looks at me again as if trying to get support for her question.

"True, but I don't want us to fall apart again when a new kid comes into the picture."

"I doubt that will happen," she shoots at me sarcastically.

"How do you know?"

"Because this one won't be a blood relative's child," she blurts out before looking up at me with wide eyes. She can't believe that came out of her mouth, and neither can I. That comment hurts. I know it sounds petty, but right now, I feel all the blame of our breakup on my shoulders. I thought we dealt with this issue; it was in the past. She stands and walks to the sink, looking out the window. I know she wants a big family; we both did. But life changes while you're living it; I thought she knew that.

My cell phone ringing breaks through the tense silence. I stare at the back of her head, willing her to turn around. When she refuses, I answer my phone.

"Steele."

"I need you in the lab. I might have found something." Victor sounds chipper for this early hour of the morning.

"I'll be right there." I stand up and head to the stairs.

"I know you didn't stay in bed last night, and I know the nightmares are back." She continues looking out the window, her back to me. "You have to talk to me or someone else or history will repeat itself."

"I'm not going to let that happen."

"If you weren't struggling, you wouldn't have a locked office in the basement."

"I promise this is different."

I head up the stairs and try to push the sound of her tears out of my head. I know she's just scared, but I'm not pulling away. Every couple has secrets, and this is mine to live or die by. I just don't know how to talk about this, not yet. She's always let me come to her when I am ready. Right now, I feel like she's pushing, and I don't know why.

***

Walking into the lab, I know Victor's going to pick apart the emotions blatantly written all over my face. As I look around the room, the refrigerator hums to its own beat, the slabs are clean, everything looks normal. I wonder if that is a good thing, this normal. Is it really normal, or is it my version of normal, which is abnormal? I think I just confuse myself.

"I should have known you were here by the smell of smoke emanating from your ears." Victor smiles as he walks past me to a small room on the other side, two coffees in hand. "You coming?" Following him into the walk-in closet, I see he's turned it into his office.

"I thought you liked being around the bodies while you did paperwork."

"Compromise to the man. I live alone in peace. I can eat and do what I please in here. They get their rules, lies about contamination, and blah blah blah." Victor hands me a large coffee before he plops his body into his new office chair. His desk is simple yet designer quality, if that is even possible.

"I thought you were a genius who didn't bow down to the powers that be."

Victor sips his coffee slowly, as if giving his brain time to think. I just watch him, his mannerisms, the way his eyes seem to focus on the nothingness of the walls.

"Just because those on high think they know better than me when I work in the trenches? They are so removed from the work they actually oversee, I doubt they would know a contagion if it was in their bloodstream eating them alive. Yet, they hold the power over budgets and my job. So, I guess simply put, even geniuses have battles to fight, Jazz. This battle isn't one of them." His attention turns to me, and I can see the depth of pain in his eyes. Unsure of what is fully causing it, my mind screams at me to find out, but I don't. It's not my place to pry. He knows if this was bigger, more criminal, I would be all over it. I leave him be because the world does not revolve around my need to know.

"Thanks for the coffee."

"You're welcome. I would have been here sooner, but they didn't believe me when I said a plain latte. It was like I was speaking a foreign language or something. Some people just like to be as boring in their lives as they are in their coffee." He smiles at me, his pain still evident, but hidden deeper.

"Well, not all of us can carry on like you and not have our asses handed to us."

"Hmm, well, that's due to my ability to deal with a dead body like no other."

"Should I be afraid of you?"

"Only if you come between me and my morning coffee concoction!"

"So, what was so important you pulled me away from my morning with Frankie?"

"You have every morning with Frankie, so be thankful for that."

Placing my coffee down on the table, I realize I am going to break my one rule with rule them all: don't pry. "You going to tell me what's going on?"

He leans back in his chair, pulls open a drawer, and tosses some papers over to me. Ignoring the fact that he almost spilled my coffee all over me, I look down at the papers. My gaze floats across the page, but the words fail to sink in. Disbelief runs through me. How is this possible when everything seemed to be okay?

"When?"

"Two months."

"What the hell, Victor! You should have told me."

"And deal with the love fest you have going on? Spare me please."

"We're your family; you should have told us."

"No, I shouldn't have. It's because we're family that I kept my mouth shut. I didn't need any of you prying into my life or trying to help me fix it. Some things are not meant to be fixed."

He's right. Some things are best to let go and move on from, even if it is something we so desperately want to hold on to. Like writing for me. I want it more than I could ever express, but I drove the road less traveled and it turned out to be a dead end. That's life.

"She move out?"

"Nope. She moved him in seeing as he's the baby's daddy."

"Where are you staying?"

"Some dive motel. I'll get it figured out eventually."

"You're staying with us."

"Right. Did you miss the part about not wanting to be around shiny, happy people right now?"

"If you think we're shiny and happy all the time, you need to lay off the funny pills from the corner store."

"Wanna talk about it?"

"This isn't about me. We're family, so get your shit together and get to the house. Chase would love some company. He needs help in science class, and maybe you understand this new addition by subtraction stuff."

"Science I'm all in, but you sic math on me, and I swear you'll wake up with a new face, no identifiable markings, no prints, and no teeth. Got it?"

"I repeat, do not piss off the guy with the medical degree."

"Among other degrees."

Seeing the light come back into his eyes a little, I turn the conversation back to the more serious nature of finding the murderer.

"Now, you going to tell me why you called me here?"

Leaning back once again, Victor pulls out a folder from the previous drawer. He tosses it on the desk toward me. This time he hits my coffee and a bit spills out. I feign my disgust with him wasting nature's most precious resource.

"Seriously, work on your aim."

"My aim is fine, thank you very much."

"For some reason, I see that as a step into the TMI area." Opening the file, I look over some notes written in what must be a new language of scribbles or chicken scratches. "What am I looking at here, Vic?"

"Mother's body was clean; nothing out of the ordinary. I mean she had several surgical scars, breast implants with serial numbers, a nose job, and a few lifts and tucks. Scars never die, no matter how small they are."

"Addicted to plastic surgery; we can check out the doctors."

"Already spoke to them when I verified the serial numbers. Well-liked and on the schedule for liposuction."

Flipping through the pages, trying to make sense of the mother's chart, I finally cave and move past it. Seeing the son's photo, I pause. The words are clearer here.

"Anything from the boy?"

"Quick, simple motion like I've told you before. No defensive wounds. No other injuries. It was just quick lights out."

Seeing Mr. Johnson's photo in the upper right-hand corner, I stop. His face looks different when not covered in blood—peaceful, almost sweet.

"Father?"

"See, this is where it gets a bit interesting." My interest piqued, I look up at Victor, who puts his stupidly expensive shoes on his desk. "Pops fought back." Flipping through the papers, I once again try to decipher the writing, but I must be dumber than a box of hammers because none of this makes sense.

"Explain?"

"His nails and left hand were broken. Nails, I would assume from trying to claw at his attacker."

"That's unusual."

"If you know you're dying, you fight like hell. That brings me to his hand; it was broken backwards. Whoever did this made sure to let dear old dad die a slow and painful death."

"Stab wounds?"

"Too many to count, and the surrounding edges too damaged to get a good impression for a knife comparison. That being said, he must have nicked himself during the barrage. I found a different blood type in the mutilation. Might help lower the pool a bit."

"Anything under the nails?"

"Nope, your assailant must have been wearing something to cover his neck completely."

"So, you're telling me that we once again have nothing to go on? Why should this case be any different?"

"Well, first, you are the detective. It's your job to find the evidence to go on; I just analyze what we have. Second, we've solved cases with nothing but a hooker's word and a dress."

"Doesn't mean it was easy."

"Nothing worth solving ever is."

"Will and I have a few things to investigate further." I stand up, finish the delicious coffee, and toss the cup in the trash. "See you at home?" Victor simply nods at me, and I leave his office.

I can tell he dislikes having to take me up on my offer. It was for the best, but he is too proud to see it. He loves his soon-to-be ex-wife too much. High school sweethearts, now defunct failures. I'm sure he'll come up with some scientific reason for the breakup beyond an affair and a pregnancy. People have always told me we are never given more than we can handle. I think those people are either mentally unstable or high all the time.

***

Walking up the steps to the private school, I feel the hairs stand on the back of my neck at those uniforms, the strict rules, and the absolute ignorance of life outside of these cement walls. Walking through the heavy double doors, Will continues to talk about something to do with his car being in the shop again. Kids run from room to room and dash from their lockers when the bell rings through the building.

"Maybe I should look into a new car? Or a used one? I never really wanted to spend the cash, ya know?" His words pull me out of my self-induced haze.

"What?"

I turn back to Will, his hand on the doorknob leading to the principal's office. "I was asking if I should buy a used or new car."

"My mother always said to buy what you could afford."

He pulls the door open, and I walk inside.

"Well, if I finance it, technically I can afford anything."

"Says the man with debt." As we walk up to the counter, I observe the place looks more like a prison than a school office. The elderly woman behind the counter wears her glasses on the top of her nose, chain attached to the sides, white hair up and wearing a cardigan sweater—your stereotypical office administrator.

"Excuse me, ma'am. I'm Detective Steele, this is my partner Detective Everts. We're here to see Principal Miller."

The woman looks over the bridge of her glasses and stares at my badge. She turns her attention to Will, and he stares blankly back. I elbow him slightly; he pulls his badge out and holds it for her to read.

"You can have a seat. He'll be with you in a moment."

Sitting in the uncomfortable metal and plastic chairs reminds me of my childhood. I was always in the principal's office. Not for being the one who started it, but always the one who finished it. Shifting nervously in my seat, my leg bounces uncontrollably.

"You look like a kid about to be suspended."

"Wouldn't be the first time."

"Should have known you were a troublemaker."

"I took bullies down a peg, after the gum was in my hair, of course."

"Ah, one of those."

"One of what?"

"The type of girl who has to finish the argument, get the last word in."

"Or knee in my case."

Will crosses his legs calmly, and I smile at his unconscious reaction. It's been nice having a partner and not having to face the underbelly of society by myself. It's different.

"My oldest is going to be in high school soon."

"You've got the gun already. You just need the earplugs."

"Forget the earplugs; I need to take the damn phone away. She acts like every text is the end of the world and she has to respond right away. Not to mention I have no idea what the new app for conversing is or if she writes in 140 characters or less. I'm at a loss."

"Welcome to modern technology. A place where crime truly can pay, and kids are the primary buyers."

He turns to look at me, a serious expression on his face. My dad had that once. It was when I told him I wanted to play baseball with the boys. It was a look of pure pride mixed with absolute fear of the ramifications of my actions. I never did play for the boys' teams—league rules and all. Softball wasn't a challenge, but what else was I going to do, knit? I was a contact girl.

"Detectives?" the woman utters over the counter, only her hair visible as she speaks. "He's ready for you." Her hair bounces as her fingers point to the room in the back left. It seems out of place, like the room was an afterthought. Kind of like when baseball teams build new stadiums and forget about the pitchers needing a bullpen to warm up. They end up putting them in foul territory, always in danger of being hit by a speeding foul ball. That's what this is right now: he's the pitcher, and we're speeding at him for information. Wonder who blinks first?

Will knocks on the door and opens it after hearing a low mumbling response. Walking in, the first thing I see are frames housing images of the principal with loads of people. In some he's holding awards, some are of just the award themselves, and others are him with famous people. This is a man who is more intent on showing who he knows as opposed to what he knows. One image jumps out at me, and my blood begins to boil—Irving Garrison with his arm around Principal Miller.

"Mr. Miller."

"Walter, please. I know why you are both here, and we've already cleaned out Miss Johnson's locker for you. Everything is here."

He lifts a box off the floor and places it on his desk.

"While we appreciate the effort, sir, we would still like to take a look at her locker."

"Yes, well, while I would love to do that, we are short lockers here, and we needed to reassign it quickly."

"So, she's gone for a few days and she's disposed of?" My voice comes out sharp and fast, like the venom from a snakebite. Will turns on his heels. I feel his eyes on me, but my brain is solely focused on the image in front of me. The principal's breathing quickens. You can hear the fear if you listen for it. I learned that from watching the good cop, bad cop interrogations. Yes, they're real, but only used on the dumbest of criminals. Normal society doesn't work that way.

"No, detective, but we have a waiting list for such commodities. Blame the budget, but do not blame me for doing right by one of my students."

"With all due respect, sir, and by that, I mean none, you were told to hold the locker for us to investigate it. We have techs that were to dust it, look for something, anything, to figure out what happened to Kaley Johnson, and you just made that a lot harder."

"Try being a principal for a week and tell me about hard."

"Walter, we're not here to cause a problem. We just want to know about Kaley's routines."

"She was a perfect student, good grades, involved in after-school activities. She was always willing to lend a hand at our fundraisers."

"With Irving Garrison?"

"If he was in attendance, yes. Although I fail to see the relevance."

"Just asking if he was there, that's all." Will watches me closely. I know he's going to be rather upset at my tone and line of questioning. There's a line we never cross, but sometimes I feel I'm entitled to teeter on it. Being shot will do that to you. The school bell rings again, and Walter stands up, brushes his shirt, and walks to the door.

"If there is nothing else, I need to get back to running the school."

Will lifts the box and walks out of the room. I pull out my cell phone and take a snapshot of the photo on the wall. Turning around, my eyes lock with Walter's. He knows who I am. He's known the moment I came into the room. He also knows I have no power here. He smiles at me as if he's got the script and I've only seen the trailer. Looking him up and down, I smile and pat him on the back before I walk by. My dad used to do that to those he thought were below him. Don't know if it works or not, but it prevents you from saying something or giving up your hand. Either that or it prevents me from losing my badge to every asshole I want to punch a smile off of.

Walking back to the car, Will is furious with me. You can tell as he walks, stomping his feet like Chase when I tell him it's bedtime. Popping the trunk, he drops the box inside, slowly flipping through its contents.

"Nothing of value's in there."

He slams the trunk. I feel like being a petulant child and saying I'm in wicked trouble now, but in this case, I know I am.

"What the fuck has gotten into you?"

"Look . . ."

"No, I don't know what's been going on in your head but get it the fuck out. You can't go in there with guns blazing because of some damn photo! For all you know, there's nothing going on there, but no, the master has to connect dots when there might not be a fucking connection!"

"He knew who I was."

"Half of fucking New York knows who you are because you were all over the news. Not every case is about them."

"Then explain emptying a locker before we got here."

"My two daughters share a locker in middle school because they don't have enough. The damn places are overcrowded, budgets suck, and don't get me started on this math addition by means of subtraction."

"Okay, so I might have overreacted."

He looks me over, the irritation slowly waning from his eyes. He pushes past me and gets in the driver's side of the car. Walking calmly around to the other side, I take one final look at the high school and realize you couldn't pay me enough to go deal with that shit again. I slide into the passenger seat, buckle in, stay quiet. Simple enough.

"You're right though, he wouldn't turn over anything to us that implicates the school." Or not.

"He's hiding something?"

"I don't know. What I do know is schools get money from grades, kids, and begging. Straight out business. Teachers are pawns. Administrators . . ."

"Satan's spawn."

Will turns the car over and laughs at me.

"I told you I was suspended a lot. I'm telling you, some of those bullies had really soprano voices when you—"

"Stop! Please, by all that is holy, stop." I stop, but the enjoyment must be plastered on my face.

"I want to check out the crime scene again, see if the techs missed something."

"Want me to come with?"

"Nah, I'll drop you off at the station."

"Frankie should have had the lawyers look over the warrant by now. I'll head to her and get Kaley's file. Make sure you check her room thoroughly. There has to be something hidden she didn't want her parents to see."

"Like what?"

"A diary about all the cute boys she wants to date."

Will pulls into the precinct parking lot. He looks at me, worry etched on his face. It's the father just realized his daughter is going to be dating soon face. He ought to be lucky he shaves his head, otherwise he'd lose his hair very quickly with worry and stress.

"You're kidding me."

Hopping out of the car, I lean down and look through the window.

"Mine had all my secrets I couldn't tell my parents. Hid it in my pillow and filled it with more cotton. Mom never found it. Shit, if she did, I wouldn't be standing, and my first boyfriend wouldn't be married with three kids."

His face pales and I shake my head, laughing at him. Closing the door, he peels out of the parking lot with a determined look on his face. Hopefully he finds something, anything to give us a clue where her body might be. I stop short. It's one thing for your mind to assume you'll never find someone, but going to body recovery is a whole different ballgame. Why did I go there? What evidence points to that? Am I connecting dots that aren't really there?

This is the hardest part of detective work: doubting your gut when you don't know why it's telling you something in the first place.

***

I've always loved the view from the office. It lets me see how small, how insignificant I am to the rest of the world. It's a blessing really, reminding yourself of this. I find myself getting lost in the fantasy of what the lives of the people below are like. Do they know there is crime happening right next to one out of four of them? Have they experienced the loss of a loved one? If I had made different choices, would any of them be in my life? I've been told to live life for myself because I am worth it, but how can one live for themselves when the world doesn't and shouldn't revolve around them?

"You lost in thought again?"

My reverie is once again broken by Frankie's calming voice. Turning, I can see her leaning on her desk, her fingers tapping on a file folder. She knows this isn't a social call. I should have called before coming here, but I was never good at keeping in touch.

"When am I not?"

"You really want me to answer that?" Her face flushes red, and I know the exact moments she's referring to. I feel the burning in my ears, and I know I must look embarrassed as hell.

"I'd rather you didn't."

She points to the couch I usually crash on, and my prior thoughts invade my mind a bit. When it comes to Frankie, focus was never my strong suit. She just assaults my mind like a great story that you never want to let go, or a good song that annoys the crap out of you. I guess it depends on what mood she's in. Forcing myself to breathe, I drag my feet to the couch, the day weighing heavy enough.

"Before we go any further, this is purely business between us. You will be able to take the copy of Kaley's file as per the warrant. That being said, please respect that I don't want to talk about this case around Chase. I understand that you might have more questions after you fully digest my notes. But please respect that just because we live together does not give you the freedom to bombard me while we are having family time. There has to be a divide between Doctor Francesca Ryan and your girlfriend when we walk out of this office."

I try to hide my smile when she uses her official title. She hates her first name; more often than not, she say it sounds like an old bat. What she won't tell you is she's named after her mother, who died when she was young. Her father called her Frankie and it stuck.

"Jasmine, are you listening to me at all?" Once again, she pulls my attention back to the task at hand. I know it's important, but I am beyond tired; it's late and there isn't enough coffee in the world to keep me going much longer. Not like I'll get sleep tonight anyway.

"Yes, I've got it and I agree."

Frankie grabs the file from her desk and holds it out for me to take. She lowers herself into the chair and motions for me to look through it. Flipping open the cover is an odd sensation. There's no photo like we normally have in our case files. There are a bunch of papers, a simple family tree of sorts, educational situation, medical jargon that I will never understand, and then I stop. I can feel the muscles tighten in my jaw, and I want to turn away from the page, but my eyes are focused on it.

"Are you sure?" My voice is so weak I don't know if she heard me. My eyes finally move upwards and lock onto hers. The sadness flows off her in waves, and I close the file in disgust. I don't want to read anymore. I know I'll have to, but right now, I can't.

She finally answers me. "Very sure. When you look through the rest of the file, you'll see medical reports backing up her claims."

"Mother?"

"Knew everything."

"This could change the entire investigation."

"It might, or it might not. I really don't know what to tell you."

"Do you think it's possible . . ." I try to find the right words, but my head is running a mile a minute. I wish the damn hamster would get off the wheel for one minute so a train of thought could form.

"I don't think she's capable of this. Based on what you told me, you want someone more precise, more professional."

"Frankie, you know as well as I do that when in that state of mind, you can do anything."

"That's very true, but Kaley would never harm her brother. In fact, she was trying to find a relative that would take them in. That doesn't sound like someone who would kill her brother."

"Maybe she didn't want him to suffer."

"That's the thing. Lester Johnson never laid a hand on his son. That was his heir apparent. The man would never harm him in any way."

"Once a pervert always a pervert."

"I tend to agree with you, but there are different classifications and desires that each individual has. He showed no interest in Daniel. It was always Kaley. Based on her rape kit, he'd been assaulting her for years. She said it started when she was thirteen. The doctors told me it was much longer than that."

"Did you report it? There was nothing in the database."

"I did and it was never entered."

"Why?"

"Kaley kept recanting. She wanted to leave, but she was terrified."

"I get that, but the kit was enough to prove it."

"Jasmine, she only consented to seeing a doctor two weeks before her disappearance. I did everything I could to get her to do it sooner, but her mother was a boar with lawyers, seeking injunctions. It's been a hell of a battle. One day Kaley shows up at my office and begs me to take her to the hospital."

"If her mother had injunctions . . ."

"I had no choice. She was bleeding and had nowhere else to go. The police and family services were heading to her house to remove both children. That's when they found the bodies."

It slowly starts to fall into place, like when you finally see the beginning of the film and the best parts of the trailer are there. Now you're not sure what to expect, but you have an idea where the train of thought is heading. Either way, I don't like it.

Chapter Four

The water droplets hit my jacket as I watch the sky light up, each drop hitting with a distinct sound, soaking in, making the clothing heavy. It doesn't matter; I feel this darkness gripping me. The rain can't wash it away. It's part of me—the guilt, the anger, the desire for revenge. I know I am my own worst enemy and can self-sabotage, but this time I feel the control leaving me. I look toward the future as much as possible, but I guess we can't ever truly outrun our past.

"You still think you're better, don't you?" I hear the voice behind me, and the hairs stand up on the back of my neck. Guilt is a funny thing. It rules you. Controls you. Hatred, that's worse.

"I thought you wanted to die so badly before. Yet, you fought back. Why?" The voice continues to hit my ears, but I ignore it . . . try to focus on the rain, the droplets, the cleansing of my soul.

"Tell me why, you stupid bitch!"

"You're not real. I know you're not. So say whatever you want, I'm going to enjoy the—" Something slams into the side of my head, snapping it harshly to the right. The ripple effect pulls me to the ground, into the mud and muck.

"Real or not, that had to hurt."

Rolling over onto my side, I hold my hand against my head. It hurts badly, but there's no blood. Shouldn't there be blood? Slowly pulling myself to my feet, I turn to see James standing there, muscles flexed, veins in his neck pumping. His eyes are black as night, his smile gone. He reminds me of the book I was forced to read in high school: *The Picture of Dorian Gray*. James was handsome in real life, but this darkness, this side of him was devoid of anything nice to look at.

A swift and painful kick to my ribs reminds me he's still there. Rolling onto my back, I take a few deep breaths, trying to control the rage building inside me. A stomp on my stomach pushes the air out faster than I can take it back in.

"You can try to ignore me all you want, but I'm here. We're all here."

Another stomp and whatever was in my stomach flies out of my mouth and onto the floor. Tears form in my eyes, but I try not to let them fall. Dreams are supposed to be safe havens; they used to be. Visiting family members, maybe a tragic situation or two, but never like this. I would relive the past, sure, but not how I am now. Something's changed, and I don't know how to stop it.

"Once you let go, it's a free-for-all."

Two hands wrap around my throat, constricting me from grasping air. My hands hang at my sides, unmoving. It's surreal. I no longer have the desire to die. I want to plan a future with Frankie and see Chase grow up, but this feeling now—it's new. The pain is deserved; the torture understood. I took a man's life, and he's haunting me.

My chest constricts, and I feel the sudden fight to breathe, but my arms still don't move. My brain is sending signals, I know it is, but they feel glued to the floor. As I stare at James, his blackened eyes want me to give in, give up. It's like this hypnotic gaze of nothingness. You either fall into it or turn away. I'm somewhere in-between. I want to turn away, but there is so much depth there. Of what I don't know. Maybe I should give in, go into the darkness and see what lies ahead. Accept that evil and use it to my advantage.

As if getting the signal from my brain, my right hand swings upwards and connects with James's head. He falls to the side of me and vanishes. Gasping for air, I pull my legs into my chest. Tears flow freely, but I ignore them. I feel the fear of letting go into that side of me. I don't want my painting to be hideous. I want to be clean. I want my conscience to be clear. Yet my heart isn't pure anymore. I've killed a man. At times like this, there is only one person in the world I want.

"Mommy," I say to the empty room around me, my voice weak, my fear evident, pain everywhere, but no matter how loud my voice seems to my ears, one thing is true. She isn't coming.

✳✳✳

Blinking my eyes, I can see the baseboard of my bedroom wall. Curled up in the fetal position on the floor, my face is tight from the tears, and my body sore from thrashing in my dreams. Forcing myself to sit up, I lean back against the headboard. My nightmares are getting worse, and I don't exactly know how to handle that. I don't want to involve Frankie in this, but I'm sure this is turning into the same fight we had when my brother died. I close up, and I know she's noticed it. I just can't worry her. Not until there's something to be worried about, right?

Pulling my knees into my chest, I try to calm myself. My mother did this a lot when she was sad or overwhelmed. She would sit on the floor, stare at the wall, eyes focused on nothing, and breathe. Deep breaths, count them if you need to. Just let them out slowly and attach the stress of the day with them. It never worked for her; her desk always piled to the nines with papers or to-do lists, but she tried.

My cell phone dances across the nightstand, and my arm seems to move on its own to grab it. My eyes glance at the screen. I know I have to answer, but I don't want to. Yet, I do.

"Steele," I say into the receiver. I hear a slight rustling sound on the other end. It sounds like Chase when he is asking Frankie what to say, even though he was calling to ask permission for something. He's gotten smart at playing us off each other. Took forever for him to to realize if one of us said no, we meant it. I love it though. It means I'm alive and living.

"Steele?" I hear through the phone, and I am reminded of where I am.

"Yeah, Will. What's up?"

"You were right about Kaley's room. I found her diary with some rather interesting passages."

"Interesting like she was complaining about her daddy issues, or interesting like you are freaking out about what teenage girls talk about?"

"Daddy issues." There's a slight pause on the other end, and I swear I can hear Will's brain working a mile a minute.

"Yes, all daughters write things in their diary that you might never know about. No, that doesn't mean you're a bad parent. Finally, no, you will not and cannot ask your daughters if they have a diary, write in one, need to talk to you about something, or whatever else is going on in that brain of yours."

"But—"

"But nothing. You don't want to do that. Keep tabs, sure, but let them come to you. Do not be the helicopter parent that hovers so much that you lose your kid. Happy medium, Will. Now, bring that thing to the house, and I'll have coffee ready."

"I'm at the office."

"Then leave it."

Hanging up the phone, I turn my attention back to my shaky hands. My grandmother had hands like mine. Mom and I always spoke about how Grandma's issues had skipped a generation and smacked me in the face. It was always a good laugh over coffee. If you make a fist, the shaking stops, but then you look like you want to punch someone out. That's what my grandmother told me. She always looked angry, but when you turned your back, she would stick her tongue out and make faces. She wasn't always angry, just in pain.

I guess getting dressed is an important thing to do before Will comes in and sees me in all my nightmarish glory. My bones, muscles, tendons, and all the other crap I never paid attention to in biology class hurt as I stand up. I wish I could just go back to sleep, but what help would that be? My brain can't shut off, and the demons in my mind take over when I can't fight them.

Getting dressed in yesterday's jeans and a new shirt, I use the bathroom. My reflection is a sad and pathetic excuse for a functioning human. At this point, makeup wouldn't cover up the dark circles or even give some color to my skin. Not like I know how to use it anyway. Just a waste of cabinet space. Not to mention being a detective and chasing down a perp in the rain is kind of hard with mascara rolling into your eyes. I'm lucky I have clean clothes at the rate I'm going. Blame the girlfriend for that, or rather, thank her.

The ringing of the doorbell signals Will is here. My ugly mug will have to do, not like I'm supposed to impress someone. Heading to the kitchen, I pull the door open and come face to face with Will, a book, and a stack of papers. Imagine a game of Jenga, with lots of loose pieces and you have to pick one, but it wobbles as you move the oxygen molecules near it. That's what Will looks like right now.

"Need some help?" I offer, but I know he'll decline. He's a man; they always decline when they need help and expect it when they don't.

"That would be great!" Or not. My understanding of men decreases by the minute, or Will is not the average male. I'll go with that. I grab some of the papers so he can actually see where he's going.

"Thanks." He walks in and drops the rest on top of my notes and Frankie's file on the table before flopping into a seat.

"No problem." I close the door. "Mind telling me what I'm looking at?"

"The life and documented times of Kaley Johnson. We found her laptop as well; tech's combing through that right now."

"Okay. Coffee?" He simply nods in response, and I grab the old coffeemaker to begin the long process of facing the day.

"There is so much in this . . . book."

"We women like to air our grievances. Most of us do it in print."

"Well, you were a girl; how did you do it?"

"Last time I checked, I still was." Laughing a bit to myself, I grab the mugs and pull the coffee out. "I played whatever sport I could get my hands on, and I wrote some short stories."

"Diary?"

"No, I was bullied badly. So it was all horror and all cathartic."

"Remind me not to upset you."

"Nah, that's all behind me. Besides, the worst bully I had was killed while trying to escape a felony."

"You don't sound too upset."

Pouring the fresh coffee into the two mugs, I think about those words. Should I feel bad? Any life lost can be tragic, but as someone who was tormented for ten years of her life, why should I feel anything? Does that make me a horrible person? I never hated the person, just really didn't want to be picked on. I never fought back with fists; it was always with words. Always personifying the behavior so I could try to understand it. I still haven't.

"I feel indifferent."

"But you said you wrote—" I cut him off by putting the mug full of piping-hot coffee in front of him. "Thanks."

"Yes, I wrote about the stupid people. I wrote about the cruel behavior, and I always made those people not have happy endings. I never killed the bullies. I didn't put their faces on the characters. It was always abstract, trying to rationalize the irrational. I don't know if I have it in me to kill . . ."

The words never exit my mouth. I do have it in me to kill someone. I already have. Mother taught me not to lie. Yet, part of me still thinks I can't kill in cold blood.

"You're not capable of cold-blooded murder, Jasmine."

I look to Will as if he was reading my mind. His eyes glaze over, and I can tell he's gone back to a place I don't ever want to visit. Yet, regardless of where our worst fears took place, we both feel the same.

"We did what we did to survive. No more, no less," he continues, sipping his coffee. Looking over the piles of papers sitting in front of us, I decide to change the subject. I don't want him to dwell on the past, even though my brain has a room there. No matter how far you move forward, some things you have done will haunt you forever. Just accept it. I do.

"So, she have a boyfriend?"

"Not that I can tell from this stuff. Would she have one at fourteen?"

"Who knows? Remember the case a month ago of the thirteen-year-old who had a virtual relationship?"

"Craigslist murder, yeah. Her parents should have been all over her though."

"Right, because it's easy to figure out who your child is texting, posting, tweeting, or whatever new thing is there. It isn't easy. You know what Jennie likes to do?"

"Cheerleading."

"Beyond that? When is she online? Who talks to her?"

His face falls a bit, and I can tell reality has hit home. It's an interesting feeling as an adult to realize you are no longer in tune with what's going on. You have to put blind faith in the people you have protected from the time they could walk. You have trust someone who has yet to truly understand the darkness the world has to offer. Sure, there's beauty out there as well, but the other side is so tempting. Like my mother said to me when I started learning how to drive, it isn't you I don't trust. It's everyone else out there. That's how I feel with Chase. He's still young, but so adult in the same breath.

"Thanks for making this a depressing morning."

"Could be worse." I shrug, even though I know in my gut the trip down the rabbit hole has just begun. This is going to get worse. Moving some papers around, I pull out Frankie's file on Kaley and hand it to Will.

He leans back to read it while I pick up the infamous teenager diary. Part of me feels like I'm violating Kaley's privacy. I know Frankie talks about writing down your feelings and letting the emotions out on the page, not in real life. I don't really write anymore. Nothing but the reports about who stabbed who and how. Besides, if I wrote a novel, I think it would be banned for containing too much gore. How else can one expect to deal with the trauma from eighteen years of torment?

Landing on one page, my heart crawls up into my throat. I feel it beating harder in my esophagus as if to choke me to death. Staring at the words, smeared by tears, I force myself to hold everything in. Force myself not to connect and go back there. Yet, I do.

"Her father?" Will's voice reeks of disgust. I simply nod, my eyes glued to the page in front of me. I hear the file hit the piles of papers, and I swear I can feel his eyes on me. "Find something?"

Taking a deep breath, I decide to read the page.

"'He did it again, worse this time. Mom was working late, Danny was sleeping. I locked my door, but he picked it. I don't know what else I can do to stop him. I've told Mom and Principal Miller. Doctor Ryan tried to help, but my mom got in the way. Grandma and Grandpa spoke to Mom, and they all think I'm dreaming this. I don't know what I'm going to do . . . I'm six weeks late."

Leaning back in the chair, I flip to the next page, but it's empty.

"She was pregnant," Will's spews like a snake spitting venom. It's harsh, angry, and filled with disgust.

Flipping through more pages, I stop on another page. The words chill me to the bone.

"'I finally had the courage. He said he'd take care of it. Danny and I will be safe. Miller will handle my father. I paid him the only way I could.'"

"You don't think . . ." Not only has it gotten worse, but we've pretty much just thrown ourselves off a cliff into a pile of smut. I can see Will is fighting his disgust.

"Yeah, I do," I state matter-of-factly. It's a classic case of abuse. No one listens. Those that try to help are bombarded with lawyers and legal jargon. In the end, a sexually abused individual feels nothing toward sex. It's a means to an end. It's payment, if it needs to be. Kaley was desperate, and that leads us to this.

"How could it get that bad? We've got laws to protect this from happening."

"Yes, but where there is a will there is a way. Even if Frankie believed Kaley, all it takes is one person saying the kid was lying and it becomes a game of he said she said."

"But Frankie—"

"It's one person on one side of the aisle. This is why I hated psychology. It isn't about helping the victim as much as it is red tape, old men with old ideas of society, and no one wanting to fix the system."

"So, they had money to hire any doctor who'd she was lying."

"And she had a mother denying the truth about what happened."

"If she wasn't dead already, I swear I'd make sure we buried her with charges."

I've seen the rage in his eyes before. Frankie held that once when we spoke about everything from our pasts—that darkness that seemed to want to take over her soul, even if there was nothing she could do. Karma has been quick and precise. Yet, she felt this intense need to exact revenge on something that was no longer an issue, at least not a living breathing one. Nightmares were a different story.

"I get it, Will, I do. But you can't let your disgust for them cloud your judgment."

He looks me over, calmly at first. I can see his mind working quickly to assess why I am not as outraged at the situation as he is. Slowly, like my mother when I told her, realization hits. He pales. He wants to say something, but I hold up my hand. This is not the time nor place for this conversation. I need to turn this back around to the case at hand.

"I think we need to have another conversation with Miller. This time down at the precinct with him in cuffs for statutory rape."

"Does she state point-blank she paid him with sex?"

"No, but we've convicted rapists with circumstantial evidence before."

It's true, we have. Doesn't mean I feel good about that statistic. Always made me queasy to think about a trial based on this type of evidence. You can mentally connect the dots, but I keep going back to experience and interpretation. What if what I see is different from what you see? What if what I see is wrong? Lots of questions that cannot be afforded to an officer of the law. We just find the evidence and try to connect the dots. Lawyers try to convince a jury of said dots, and the people vote to see if it holds up.

Will's cell phone rings and he grabs it. Staring at his face, I know something's up, but my mind wanders to the court of public opinion. If this case gets out there, we will be raked over the coals for not protecting her. Frankie will be called everything under the sun for no apparent reason. Her degree, her professionalism, her personal life will all be spoken about online. No filters, no responsibility, and no lawyers to present all sides equally. Just groups of random strangers screaming about how she should be punished. Sadly, I can see all the negatives clear as day, pointing to her sinful ways clouding her ability to be a good doctor. My skin crawls at the thought. She's an amazing woman who followed the law, but that doesn't matter when people are hurt. You will always be to blame if the outcome isn't what the public wants. What scares me is the fact that I cannot stop it or protect her or Chase from it. I'm helpless against the control some fool anonymously has from the comfort their living room. I am a control freak, and I cannot do a damn thing.

"We have to go." My eyes meet his once again, and my gut screams at me. I know what he is going to say before he speaks.

Kaley's been found.

***

The park is beautiful this time of year. The snow has long since melted, but the evidence it was once here lies in the lush grass. The slight hill ahead reminds me of the days my brother and I would roll down them in a race with no clean winner. Who could call out 'I win' when you couldn't stand up or see straight? Those memories still bring a smile to my face and a warmth to my heart. I should bring Chase to the park one day, tell him about those days gone by.

As I get closer to the greener tree though, my smile fades and my heart sinks. I don't want to share this pain with anyone. It's time to close off to the world and focus on what's in front of me.

"How long?" I ask Victor as he approaches me.

"Less than ten hours, but I'll know more after I do a full exam." His eyes are empty and lost. My own must look the same. Except mine must be gray; they always change when I'm hiding my emotions. Pushing past him, my feet drag me to the base of the tree. I hear Will's and Victor's footsteps as they follow behind.

Kaley sits, legs crossed, arms folded on her lap, makeup on and hair styled. She looks like a beauty pageant contestant, perfect in every detail down to the pressed school uniform. Leaning down, I grab a latex glove from my jacket pocket and snap it on. I move her hair slightly, revealing her neck. No signs of strangulation. No bruising. Nothing.

Pulling her lips apart, I see her mouth is empty, her teeth clean. Sliding up the hem of her skirt, the bruising begins to show itself. Moving it up further, it's evident she was sexually assaulted recently. Pulling the clothing down to hide the violence, I look around the area. Wide open. No cameras. Loads of people who are busy with their families. In other words, no witnesses.

"Will, maybe you should visit Mr. Miller at work. See if we can get a search warrant for his place with what we've got."

He simply nods at me, and his expression is full of thanks. He'd stay if I asked him to, but why bother. All he sees right now are his little girls.

I don't care how hardened a Marine he used to be. He's a father. Once you're a parent, scenes like this change radically.

"Who has the balls to dump a body in one of the most exposed areas of the park?"

"One who wants her to be found quickly," I mumble to Victor. He's struggling with this one. Everyone had hoped Kaley would be found alive. That is the best and worst thing to have as a human being—hope. I never had it for her. Facts, human behavior, and experience made that decision apparent before we even had an accurate timeline.

"So, they had to respect her, right?"

"No, a self-respecting human being doesn't rape and kill a young woman before her life has a chance to start."

"You know what I meant."

I stand in front of Victor, my jaw set, muscles tight.

"No, I don't know. This wasn't about respect. It was about control. It was about ownership. Whoever did this wanted to preserve her exactly as they saw her. This has nothing to do with respect. No assault does."

Victor looks me over, his eyes searching mine for some reason behind my outburst. I give him nothing. My poker face forces him to step back.

"If you're done here, I'll take the body back to my lab."

"Call me if you find anything." He walks over to his team, and I watch as they move Kaley from the tree. Several officers stand by me as if waiting for some instruction on what to do. Time to be a hard-assed cop with no emotions.

"Canvas the area, find out if anyone here saw something, don't talk to the press, and find me something to go on!"

My stern voice causes them to scatter quickly, some out of fear of me, others because they would rather be walking in a park than dealing with my ego. I can't blame them. Looking around the park, you can see the satellite poles for news vans. The vultures are here waiting to pick apart the story. Put it everywhere. Sometimes the idea of the people needing to know makes me fucking sick. I wish I didn't know half of what I did, and knowing Chase is exposed to all of this at a young age angers me.

As a parent, you can only block out so much before your kid goes to school and some other child with assholes for parents shows him everything you wanted hidden. It's wrong. It's despicable. It's inevitable. How can you teach right from wrong when you commit rape in a video game for points? Seeing all the families in the park just reminds me how outnumbered we are. One out of five of those girls will be sexually assaulted in their lifetime. No video game, movie, or television show will change that, but the reporting goes down. Kids get desensitized to what they see daily. No outrage, more scrutiny of victims and what they did, less chance of a conviction. It's a cycle that no one can break.

"Detective?"

A young man stands in front of me with a cell phone in his extended hand.

"I'm sorry to bother you, detective, but the tech lab wants to speak with you."

"Why didn't they call my phone?"

"Umm, they did, ma'am, but you weren't answering."

"So, they called you, Officer . . ." What the hell was his name?

"Pevy, ma'am. My brother works in the lab and asked me to come find you."

"Right. Well, thank you."

As I grab the phone out of his hand, he steps a few paces back to give me space. "Steele," I say into the receiver while my eyes focus on the officer in front of me. He seems to find the grass fascinating.

"Detective, this is Logan from the tech lab. I found some interesting things on Kaley Johnson's laptop. I think you ought to come down here."

"On my way."

Disconnecting the call, I hand the cell phone back to the waiting officer. Patting him on the back, I walk away and hear him exhale loudly. Trying not to let him hear me, I stifle a laugh. Even in these situations, laughter is always the best medicine. It might be horrible of me, but damn I love how the newbies are afraid of anyone in power. Kind of like my grandmother was to me. It didn't matter that she had osteoporosis; one swift kick to my shin, and she had access to smack me in the head. Good times.

Walking into the technology lab is like walking into another world. Wall to wall monitors, dimmed lights, room temperature at a chilly degree, and rows of desks. The constant clicking on keyboards and mice and the mumbling to themselves or one another is what hits my ears first. The movements are rushed; you can feel the tension here. The low hum of the ventilation unit catches my ears as I wonder what my brother would think of all this. He was a technology geek; if it was new, he had it. You name the Apple device, he had it, broke it, and found a way to fix it again. Me, I wish I could type my reports on my old typewriter with corrective tape. It was my dad's, and it was old as shit, but it never got infected. Well, it did once, but that was due to the tiny human currently in my care.

"Detective Steele?"

Turning around, I come face to face with a well-dressed, muscled man. His glasses gently hug his nose as his arms fight against the fabric of his button-down shirt, his hand outstretched for me to take.

"You must be Mr. Pevy." I shake his hand and am surprised by the firm, yet gentle handshake. My father, for all of his faults, told me that a man's handshake was his bond. It showed his character. Weak or fake handshake, poor human being. Those with strong but gentle handshakes, like Will and Mr. Levy here, they tend to be good men. Too strong, controlling bastard. Same goes for hugs. I wish I'd paid attention to this when I was younger.

"Please, call me Logan. I'm sorry for having my brother bother you. I know how rookies can be annoying as hell when they first start."

"Not a problem. I never had a reason to come down here before."

"Most detectives don't want to come down here. It's against everything you're trained to look for." He replies.

He motions with his hands for us to start walking. I fall in line with him as we weave through the desks of space aliens. They have to be some kind of aliens to be able to figure out that code or whatever it is.

"I think my training has treated me well."

"Of course, detective. I meant nothing hurtful by it. It's just this is not what you're used to. Sure, we track bank statements, cell phones, and what not, but that doesn't warrant a trip here. What you have, you're going to need us for. Me specifically."

He pushes open his office door, and I walk into what could be a replica of Chase's bedroom. Every shelving unit has some kind of action figure on it, and the logos of Batman and Superman hang on the wall. Behind his desk, a full-length autographed poster of Hadley, a knife behind her back, leans up against a wall.

"You a Hadley Moreno fan?"

"You could say that. I met her at a convention in Boston about eight months ago. She's great." Logan grins.

Sitting in a chair opposite his desk, I smile to myself. Leave it to Hadley to make an amazing impression on someone. Logan's smile was authentic, reaching his eyes. That being said, he keeps playing with his hands, and that makes me nervous. What is he hiding from me?

"So, why am I going to need you on this case?"

He leans back in his chair, his smile suddenly gone and his eyes serious.

"Kaley left an obvious trail in her search history. Normally kids purge it after every search, but you can tell she was in a hurry. She hadn't run a test on her computer for a long time."

"Forgive my ignorance, but what does her testing have to do with her searches?"

"Kaley ran a test every month to ensure her computer was running at peak performance. Her chat logs, video chats . . . everything was always purged so her searches weren't traceable. Every kid does it, yet the last month, she seemed to not care. The computer was sluggish, and her search history was available for anyone to see."

"Okay, so what was she searching for?"

"A hit person."

"Murder for hires? Where the hell do you search for that?"

"Well, her initial searches were through Google, but no single human specifically shows up. However, one person recommended a program and an explanation on how to access it."

"You lost me. Someone contacted her to tell her to download a program that could kill someone?"

"Sort of. She posted on a support forum for abused teens asking for help in getting away from her parents. Someone private messaged her with the name of a program. She was to install it and use the specific code he provided. It gave her access to the dark web."

"And what is that?"

"Basically, an untraceable area of the internet where you can buy everything from drugs to young children to a hit person for hire."

"The government has no way to track any of this?"

"We do and we don't. We have Kaley's laptop, and she saved the password, so I can access it until her account is closed."

"Who would close it?"

"Whoever gave her access in the first place. This is the most difficult type of crime in the word to track and prove."

"Can you search for someone on there?"

"No, everything is communicated through anonymous names. Money changes hands after it's bounced through a ridiculous number of IP addresses. So far all I have found is that she was in constant contact with a D.B.M. His IP is pretty much hidden."

"Was she hidden?"

"Once she downloaded that program with that specific access code, it creates a unique and untraceable IP. The whole idea of the dark web is to ensure anonymity."

"So, no one from that world could come here and kill her."

"I didn't say that. I just know they couldn't trace her through it. It's extremely difficult."

"This makes me even more paranoid about Chase having his own computer."

"My niece wanted an iPhone. She's eight; I gave her one recoded to only allow emergency calls and previously programmed games."

I laugh. "She must love you."

"She said she wanted an iPhone; she didn't say anything about the full use of one."

"Let me know if you find anything else. I promise to answer this time."

"You know, Hadley is at the convention center this week. If you're a fan of hers, maybe stop by and say hi."

"Maybe I will, thanks."

I shake his hand once more before heading out the door. If I knew half of what he did, my kid would be locked in a panic room, taking classes online with tunnels to a park with his friends. Hell, maybe I'd just build an underground fortress and hide all the kids I know there. Razors in candy, sure, but my mother never dealt with this shit.; Villains in an untraceable space where no one can find or catch you? Fuck no.

***

Walking down into the pit of the precinct with a bottle and two plastic cups, I feel the weight of everything bearing down on me. My body finds its way to Victor's office, dropping into the chair furthest from the door. I always have to keep my back to a wall. Some things never change. Filling one of the plastic cups to the top, I lean back in the chair.

Drinking the harsh fluid, I feel it burn all the way to my stomach. Means I'm still here. I can still feel things. Still haven't touched the Garrison angle in this whole case. I want to, God I want to, but there's not enough to get the captain to loosen his grip. He won't let anyone go near Irving and his company without ample piles of paper. I'm so tired of this fight.

"Come here to apologize?"

Victor stands at the door, his arms folded, defensive. I simply pour him a plastic cup full of liquid fuel. He sits back and takes a sip. His eyes widen when he realizes its Johnny Walker Blue Label. Smiling, he sits back and slowly sips the scotch. The bottle sits on his desk, half empty from our two lone pours. Last time I had this was with my brother after Mom died. We finished the whole bottle. It's only for special occasions and not of the fun variety.

"What's going on, Jazz? You're on edge, your eyes look like hell, and you pull out the Blue card?" he drawls, and I just lean back, put my feet up on the corner of his desk, and drink.

"Is it because Frankie wants a bigger family?" My eyes catch his, and he nods in understanding. He knows I don't want a repeat of the "Chase fiasco" as we've called it in the past. He also knows I think about everything from stress to money to college. Hell, I'm already planning ahead to Chase's wedding. I plan everything I can whenever I can. Frankie and I can plan when to have a kid, but the rest I have to give up control of—again.

"I'm just not ready for that, and I don't know how to tell her."

"Have you tried 'Frankie, I'm just not ready yet.'"

"She pulled the 'we're not getting any younger' card."

"You aren't, but there are always going to be kids in foster care who need a good home."

"Maybe."

"Jasmine, you are wonderful with kids. You and Frankie are great parents to Chase. You both know that, so please drop the act and talk to me about what's really going on."

Okay, how to start the conversation I don't want to have.

"Tell me about the body."

Just don't start at all.

"Sexual trauma, lots of it. She was bound and gagged, probably for the majority of the time she was missing."

"Cause of death?"

"Asphyxiation."

"Weapon of choice?"

"Based on the feathers in her throat, down pillow would be my guess."

"Anything else? DNA?"

"No, but we got a good print from her thigh. Got a hit on the first try."

"Walter Miller." It was a fact, no question in my voice. I knew he had taken her; the diary told me. The bigger question is why kill Daniel.

"Will was sitting at the house waiting for him to come home."

"He didn't tell me."

"You're sitting in my office drinking. I doubt you paid attention to your phone."

"Right."

"You're off your game."

I'm not just off my game; my piece has fallen off the chessboard. I've got nothing to add to that. I just nod and drink. It's easier. I don't trust my voice.

"Case hits close to home, doesn't it?"

"Just reminds me of Dennis. The things . . ." I take a big gulp of the liquor and cough a little. One wrong phrasing, and I know the tears will pour out of my eyes. I don't want to be weak, but lack of sleep and this case are causing my raw emotions to come to the surface.

"What things, Jazz? He was a dick, and luckily you ditched him before going to college."

"My brother made him break up with me."

"Henry? Why would he do that?"

Gulping down the rest of the scotch, I can hear Henry screaming at me in my head. *Sip it. Don't chug!* Taking a few breaths, I focus on my hands. They're more entertaining when you're about to bare your soul.

"Dennis didn't like who I was. All during high school, and especially our last year together, I was his girlfriend. I wasn't Jasmine Steele; I was Dennis Frank's girlfriend. I was branded with jewelry, keychains, held onto tightly every time we went to one of his frat parties."

Pouring more liquor into my cup, I know I'm well on my way to getting drunk. There are so many emotions swirling inside me, and I don't want to feel any of them. Victor just watches me, pity etched on his face. I hate that.

"He said he accepted me as I was though. Told me that he didn't care about my bisexuality, as long as I was faithful to him. I never cheated on him. Never even thought about it, but during the third year of our relationship, things changed. I enjoyed being out, playing on a baseball team. Hell, I remember hitting the ball further, and it irritated him so much. Here was his girlfriend showing him up, living her life, and not catering to him. His parents hated me and despised the fact that I didn't bend over backwards for him. I was a freshman in college, trying to find my way in the world, and they wanted me to be a wife. I loved him, I did, but I wasn't ready for that. I wasn't ready for everything being a wife entailed."

"I'm not understanding why Henry would get involved if these issues were the problem. I know all of this, and that's why everyone who met him pretty much thinks he's a dick."

"I hadn't slept with him."

"Jazz, we both were there for the drunk truth or dare. We know your first was some hot-ass blonde guy with an accent in your twenties." He chuckles as he drinks. It's obvious the alcohol is hitting him. Sadly, this conversation is sobering me up.

"I let him have it, Victor. I was terrified he was going to leave. He was getting forceful, and I just stopped fighting. It was easier to let your mind wander. Hurt like a bitch, but the bruises would fade with time. He was the first person I ever loved; my self-worth was wrapped up in him, ya know?"

He nods in response, but his look of pity breaks me. The tears slowly roll down my cheeks, the alcohol helping my defenses fall.

"I wish I had more strength to push him off, continue to scream no, whatever I could. We don't get that ability. No one believes us. It's what a girlfriend is supposed to do. It depends on what I was wearing and what not. So, I get why Kaley was struggling. I was desperate for help, but I felt responsible for the whole thing. My mother had no idea, but Henry—he knew. He went with me to the doctor. You are willing to do dark things when pushed to that point."

"Does Frankie know?"

"Yeah. It's funny that she was the only one who could make the nightmares stop. She helps when I wake up crying; she made me feel human again. Then I go and almost lose her anyway when Henry dies and leaves Chase with me. Everything leads back to the kids, huh?"

Victor laughs as he grabs the bottle and pours more in his cup. He taps on his phone for a few seconds and then turns his attention back to me. The pity seems to have faded and a slight brightness fills them.

"See, this is what makes you a good cop. You think of the victims and the perps. You remember what it was like to go through something similar; you have a connection to it all. Yet, you can disconnect when you have to. You can be calculating and cold if it's called for. That makes you who you are. Kids aren't gonna change that."

"I need to deal with some things first."

"Stop obsessing about the connections to Garrison and focus on the little things. If the case is there, it'll be there. Don't lose yourself trying to force things, Jazz. If he fucks up, he fucks up. You can't make it happen."

"I could, but then I'd be sleeping on the couch for the rest of my life. Frankie doesn't like meanies."

"Because mean people do mean things to innocent people. May I ask what brought this on?"

Looking at the door, I see Frankie in all her beauty. Smiling wildly, I know I am three sheets beyond the wind. Victor looks no better than I, and before I can control it, I'm in a fit of giggles. Looking over at Victor, he's struggling, and I know it. Within seconds, he's lost as well, the two of us giggling idiots while Frankie looks on, confused as hell.

It's then that it hits me like a freight train: life can be good. Right now, it is.

Chapter Five

M y wall of wonder teases me as I'm no closer to understanding any-thing. The strings feel pointless, like I've crafted a web for creation's sake. Pulling out a copy of Johnson's identification badge and Miller's photo, I hang them on the board. Well, I stab them with thumbtacks to an already crowded miscellaneous section of my wall. They're connected, but I don't know how, and I'm beginning to lose my edge.

Gulping down my water to swallow some pills helps me keep my hangover at bay. I don't even know if Victor remembers texting Frankie, but I'm glad he did. No way were we driving home. Well, I might have tried but would have failed miserably. Sitting here in this room, I know life is good. I want to find the connection. I want to get this off my chest. Yet, in the same breath I don't want to. I just want to walk away.

"You could you know."

I'd know that voice anywhere. It's the calm, soothing tone that always made the bad dreams go away. I'd wondered when my imagination would bring her back, but I'm not dreaming this time. Sleep deprivation must be taking its toll.

"It's that among other things." Turning around, I see my mother in her youthful glory. I want to reach out and touch her, but let's be honest: this isn't real. I'm not dumb, and Lord knows I am not blind, but this isn't real.

"Why are you here?"

"I don't know. You talked to your grandfather growing up; why would I be any different?"

"Grandpa died when I was a kid."

"And your imagination allowed you to talk to him. It's not a bad thing; this is just how you deal with things. What did Frankie tell you? You create scenes in order to understand and decipher the problem."

"Nightmares."

"Well, you do have those, and you should talk to her about them. This not so much; you are talking to me because you want to, not because I'm here. You could have picked your brother, Belinda, your father, or grandmother. Whomever you felt would help you figure this out."

"Crazy. Yup, I'm nuts."

My mother's body shakes as she erupts with laughter, a sound I have always loved.

"Jasmine Marie Steele, you are not crazy. You're just not like everyone else. Stop being stubborn and just realize your imagination created me so you can figure this out."

"During waking hours . . ."

"You're stressed and haven't been sleeping. Need I say more?"

"Point taken."

My mother stares at the walls, at my web of disconnect. I can see the displeasure on her face. If she was alive, I'm sure she'd be scolding me about something. Maybe the color of my string is wrong. Maybe I am missing what is right in front of my face. I truthfully don't know. I'm seeing my mother in living color, so I don't know if I am a good judge of anything right now.

"You've done so much work here."

"Yeah, but it isn't enough."

Her hand follows the green lines. Then they fall on a picture of Henry, Belinda, and Chase. Her fingers trace the outline like I've done so many times before.

"You still blame yourself?"

"No, been there done that. This isn't about guilt."

"Vengeance, then."

"Partially. It's also my way of bringing someone to justice. You're not supposed to make money off your crimes, yet Irving Garrison did and continues to do so."

"So many people commit crimes every day. People make money off the backs of slaves everywhere. How can you save them all?"

"I can't."

"Then let this all go. Dealing with this is becoming an addiction for you. It's disrupting your sleep, bringing up nightmares you left behind months ago. Jasmine, you are beyond obsessed."

"This is where I tell my mother, who is a figment of my insanity, to just back off."

"You know he'll make a mistake, and then you catch him. Until then, live your life."

"I do."

"No, you don't. You simply exist during the majority of it. You have moments, but mostly you exist."

Those words hit me in the chest hard. They were the exact words I said to her almost every day toward the end of her life. I know people say you become your parents, but this is not someone I want to be. I am just doing my job, and my own second guessing is going to cause issues. Looking back up at her, I realize I'm once again alone, the image having done its job of placing seeds of doubt in my already cluttered mind. The vibration of my cell phone pulls my attention.

"Steele."

"I'm outside. We've got another body." Will's voice cuts through the tension in my soul. Hanging up the phone, I gather my thoughts before heading into the unknown.

***

Walking up the grassy knoll, I'm brought back to my father talking about Kennedy and political conspiracies. I can just imagine him walking up to the yellow tape and damning authority. He never liked those in power. Unless it was my mother. Then he respected it. Never underestimate a woman who cleans your underwear or cooks your food. I learned that from my mom and *Murder She Wrote* reruns.

"What have we got?" I ask as my feet drag me to stand beside Victor near the coroner's van. He looks up at me, and for the first time since I've known him, he looks green. I've seen it before after a gallon of tequila and a pound of lemons and salt, but this is different. My head begins to hurt at the prospect of what I'm about to face.

"Male, mid-fifties, Caucasian . . . "

"You're very down to business today," I throw at him, hoping he'll take the lead and explain why he looks like shit.

"Yea, well. There's not much for me to do here."

"Cause of death?"

"Pretty clear."

I've always considered Victor to be a well-rounded, good-looking, dark-skinned male. I'd never date him, because that would be like dating my brother. He's part of my other family, if you will, and right now I see a man with disgust written on his face.

"Vic . . ."

"I took an oath when I became a doctor. Didn't matter the position of the graduate from best in class to barely doctor, we all took the same oath with the same wording. In essence, we remember that we are treating human beings, not disorders or diseases. We help, not harm."

I watch him fight for his words, slowly pulling them out of his mind one at a time. It's a bit funny what he's said though. I know that as long as you pass the classes, you're a doctor. I sat in the emergency room once waiting on X-rays for my foot. The doctor came to me, told me my wrist was sprained, and I could go home. He ignored my attempts to prove him wrong and discharged me. I guess regardless of oaths, all people inevitably cause harm.

"Everyone is capable . . ."

"Of being a bastard. I know that, Jazz. But this . . . this was a brutaliza-tion of a man by someone with medical training."

"Okay, so there's an evil doc running around killing people. Doesn't mean you need to take it personally. There are bad cops, horrible aunts, and don't get me started—"

"This isn't about you, dammit!" He punches the van, and his eyes harden. I've never seen him like this before, and frankly, I never want to again. Either way, right now I want to smack him, but as an adult I won't. Who am I kidding? As an adult, I would easily punch him. As a friend, I will back off.

Turning to the crime scene, I duck under the tape as Victor calls after me. I have no patience for other people's crap. I know I'm being a bitch right now, but it is what it is. As I stand next to Will, he's frantically writing notes down, but I can't read his scribble. His shorthand is worse than Chase trying to do common core math. Neither one makes any bit of sense.

"Victor say anything?"

"Male, Caucasian, mid-fifties, and cause of death would be pretty clear once I saw the body."

"He's right."

Will points to the body, and I get my first glimpse of the victim. It looks like a body, kind of. There's no trail of blood leading to him. Body dump then. No evidence of a struggle, supporting the whole body dump thing. Seeing the body up close makes my stomach turn. I've seen a lot in my life, but this is something out of one of Hadley's movies.

Walter Miller, eyes closed, lies on his back, arms out, palms to the sky. His glasses are perched on his face as if he fell asleep reading, his skin pale. His hands and arms show no defensive wounds. All things I've seen before. Kneeling down, I look at the damage before me, and my coffee decides to make a second appearance.

Swallowing the acid back down, I snap on a pair of latex gloves. I need to see this. Call it morbid curiosity, call it inquisitive, call it whatever the hell you want. His shirt was cut down the center, and not like a great eighties cutoff. This was done with a set of scissors or something similar; it's clean a cut. The cut on the skin looks the same: clean, precise, perfect.

As a kid, you always put your hands into things. If there's a cake, there are fingers swiping some icing. Mud pies, the garden, or, in the case of my brother once, dog poop. It's natural that we always put our hands in things. It's how we learn about texture and make a connection to whatever we're touching. As adults, we know when to stick our hands in something and when not to. Right now, I really don't want to, but the stupid in me wins out, and I do.

Nothing. I feel nothing. Pulling my hand out suddenly, I fall on my ass. So much for the not washing jeans movement. Rest assured my ass is green, and not with envy, as I release my stomach full of coffee onto the lawn beside me.

"At least you kept it away from the body. Two newbies splashed a bit too close."

Looking up at Will, I see him stronger than ever, calm, stomach still full from breakfast. Part of me wants to ask him how that's possible. Maybe there's a class you can take: How Not to Puke at a Crime Scene 101. Yet, I know why he's okay. He's seen men blown to pieces, men trying to hold their intestines in while waiting for help. He's seen worse, and I must look like a weak private to him right now.

Snapping my gloves off, I stand up and try to catch my bearings. If I don't think about the fact that my mouth tastes like ass, I'll be okay. Then again, how do I really know what ass tastes like? And I succeed in making myself hurl whatever didn't come out of my mouth before. I hear Will chuckling in the background. Damn him and his Marine genes.

"You done yet?"

Using my sleeve, I wipe my mouth, then scrunch up my nose at the action. Now I'm gonna smell like bad puke all day. I need a shower and a new cup of coffee. Maybe a latte; since I threw it up, the calories from my morning coffee don't count. I can rationalize anything I want really.

"Jasmine, you done?"

"Yeah, just thinking."

"They still count."

"What?"

"Just because you threw up the majority of it, the stomach was already digesting it."

"And this is where I say stop reading my mind, scary Marine man."

"No witnesses in the area and no evidence of nibbling."

"So he hasn't been here long."

"Not according to Victor, no."

"Why the same park as Kaley?"

"This is a bit more secluded, so they didn't want him to be found quickly."

"Yet, we did because . . ."

"Early morning jogger. Said she normally doesn't take this path, but wanted to try something different."

"Kaley was by the kids' area in the tree dividing the baseball field from the tiny humans."

"Miller was left in the wooded area that is rarely traveled."

"Yea, but you and I both know we would have found the body eventually. It's not like he's buried or even folded up and disposed of. The man has no organs inside of him; I'm sure he could have been disposed of in a different way. Why leave him here where he will be found at some point?"

"Comfort."

The word sends chills down my spine. Comfort to me is hanging out on a really nice couch with Frankie and Chase watching a movie. Comfort is an amazing cup of coffee. Comfort is not a place to dump bodies. Hell, the whole point of killing people is to get away with it. This is not getting away with it. This is taunting the police to see whose ego is bigger.

"Chase plays lacrosse here."

The words sound foreign to me. Small, empty, like when I spoke to my brother while he was slowly dying. Nothing had meaning. Grabbing my cell phone, I call Frankie.

"Hey, honey. What's up?"

"I don't want Chase going to any more lacrosse practices. Or games. Or play dates in the park. No more park. Nothing. I don't care."

"Okay," she says, drawing the words out slowly. She thinks I'm nuts. Considering I left my basement after seeing my mother who is long dead, I would question it myself. "Mind telling me why?" she asks simply.

"Murderer dumping ground," I flatly reply. I can't add emotion here, otherwise I will be dry heaving for the next couple of hours.

"Okay then. No park for the foreseeable future."

"Thank you." I disconnect the call before letting her ask me anything else. I know her well enough to expect a barrage of questions concerning this case, everything from who he is to who did it. In other words, everything we all want to know, and nothing I can answer. I wonder if I could sing "one of these things is not like the other" and the information would magically appear. Man, sometimes I wish I was young and didn't have to deal with killers and their idiocy. Or psychotic behavior . . . Then again, kids in high school are no better. I guess this is the lesser of two evils.

Florescent lights illuminate the small house. The wallpaper reminds me of the disco era when my mother thought my brother wanted to dress in vertically striped pants with a bright shirt. He was four; he had an excuse. My father had a matching outfit; he should have known better.

Touching the plastic-covered furniture, I can hear my mother yelling at my brother and me to stay out of the living room, a chain dividing us from the Promised Land where GI Joe and Care Bears could roam free. A place where holidays were held and a massive stereo unit with a record player and an eight track unit resided. I swallow the memory-sized lump in my throat.

"You okay?"

"Yeah," I lie. I don't need memories right now. "Just reminds me of my parent's house before they renovated." Trying to keep it light, I feel detached. Like I am following this case, but it feels outside of me. Yet, in the basement, everything connects somehow.

"We've got people all over the house looking for anything about this case."

"Tech already grabbed the laptop and headed back to the nerd cage."

"It's not so bad down there."

"I know nothing about the cave except that is where my brain cells go to die. I don't get it, and I don't care to. Point and shoot, remember?"

"Sounds like a personal problem."

I walk past Will and head down the stairs into the basement. Leave it to movies, novels, and other psychology books to insist the basement is the best place to house all the evidence. Between the dampness, dimly lit rooms, and the smell, you'd think a criminal would want to take better care of their evidence.

Debris litters the floor; everything from old books to clipped floor tiles cover as far as the eye can see. This is why criminals like the basement so much. It's away from prying eyes, and people who don't like it. Yet, to them, it's where they can be who they are.

"I hide in the basement . . ." I mumble to myself. Am I like them? Is that what my nightmares are trying to tell me? I'm no better than those who hide little girls in basements. I punch the wall. Or more accurately, through the wall to Walter Miller's secret hideaway.

"Will!"

He comes down the stairs, skipping every other step. I pull some more sheetrock out of the way, and he peers inside. He starts to tap the wall, and the sounds change oddly. He places his ear to the wall while I continue to work on removing the obstacle.

"Would be faster if you helped me."

He smiles and pushes the wall hard. It clicks and opens.

"Or you could do that. Have I mentioned how your military training makes me look bad?"

"No, but I'll make sure to let the Marines know."

"Funny, really."

I walk around him, my flashlight illuminating the obsession with Kaley Johnson and other young female students.

"He must have had cameras hidden everywhere."

"There must be hundreds of photos here. How the hell did he not slip up?"

"Maybe he didn't act on it."

I turn and see Will standing over a makeshift sink with a few bottles lining the circumference. Picking one up, I see no label, but it smells hideous. In a split second, I gag and force my stomach to keep its contents.

"What the hell?"

"No idea, but this makes me wonder if he ever touched any of those girls."

"He finally took a step into the darker side though. Kaley comes to him with a desperate plea for help," I say, thinking out loud.

"He can finally enjoy all his fantasies through her payment," Will adds as it all seems to fall into place.

"Until he finds out she's pregnant."

"Destroys his illusion, and he kills her."

"Making her look like a beautiful doll for us to find."

I dry heave again, causing Will to take a step back. He points to the stairs, and I can tell he wants to get rid of me. Can't blame him; shoes are expensive.

"I'll keep the techs working and make sure this gets a thorough onceover. Go see if Victor is calm enough to share any findings."

Afraid to open my mouth to say anything, I simply smile, turn, and rush out of the basement. I swear I can feel my stomach fighting me with every step. That's it; I need military training for my stomach. Leaving my DNA all over the place is really not professional.

***

I find myself back in Victor's morgue hoping for more information. Anything has to be better than what we found at Miller's house. Beyond wanting to leave my lunch again, I want to hurt this man. If he wasn't already dead, I know I would want to put him in gen pop. Pedophiles don't do well in the general population. Even criminals have a code of ethics; children are off-limits.

"Penny for your thoughts?" Victor smiles at me from his perch on the wall.

"I think with inflation that might be a bit cheap."

"Nah, whatever's going on in that mind of yours is not worth much." He smiles, the earlier confrontation seemingly forgotten.

"Feeling better?"

I can see his face fall into an unreadable expression. I know he's upset about the situation, and you always lash out at the ones you love most. Trust me, I wrote a book on that once. He pushes off the wall and saunters over to me.

"I sort of am."

"Drinking?"

"Overdosing of sorts."

"On what?"

He holds up his hand, holding a rather large chocolate bar. Most men would go for drugs, liquor, or spending sprees, but not Victor. He runs for the candy bars. No wonder he and I get along. One of the worst fights we ever had was over a Whatchamacallit. He wanted it. I got it. Never underestimate a woman and her desire for chocolate.

"I remember a time when you would buy some rather expensive items when you needed to deal with the stress."

"Ah yes, well chocolate is cheaper, and since the soon-to-be ex-wife is trying to bleed me dry, this is all I could afford."

"Anything I can do?"

"Not hold my little outburst against me?"

"It's forgotten."

"So what brings you down to the depths of my own personal hell?"

I stare at him blankly. I want to answer the obvious, but truthfully, why the hell would I be here if not to discuss the victim? His eyes search mine for a few seconds before the synaptic responses in his brain start to connect the dots.

"Oh, Walter Miller, right? Yes, no organ man."

"Whoever did this did us a favor. Less man hours needed to convict him. Less tax dollars at work."

"Well, that is point one. He did have sexual intercourse with Kaley Johnson. No protection was used."

"Can you tell how long ago? She wrote in her diary she paid him for helping her deal with her family issue."

"Then it had to be more than once. The evidence was dried and located on his underwear and his genitals."

"What about the obvious missing organs?"

"Before we go there, he had a wound on the back of his head. Leads me to believe blunt force trauma is the cause of death."

"Considering the condition of the body, one would assume blood loss."

"If he wasn't already dead, yes, that would most likely be the reason. There is something a bit more disturbing. There's evidence in the esophagus that Mr. Miller was kept alive."

"Why?"

"I think that would be obvious. He was to be harvested. I found some bone removed and replaced by cheap PVC pipe."

"Let me get this straight. Someone killed him and kept him alive just to take his bones and organs?"

"Yes, the black market has many buyers for this kind of thing."

"Okay, so what kind of person would be buying?"

"Someone who is on the transplant list, someone who is ineligible, parents desperate for their children, people looking to make money."

"Ineligible people?"

"Alcoholics, drugs addicts, those who are too sick or not sick enough. There's a lot of paperwork, politics, and money involved."

"So, people will turn to another source, even if the risks are high."

"Usually those whose organs are used or harvested have type O blood. The universal donor. Mr. Miller was type A."

"You lost me."

"There have been several cases of organ harvesting where the individual is stalked and hunted down for their body parts. In most cases, the victim's medical history is hacked before the abduction. If they are type O, they go missing within a matter of days. Then you promote you have the organs and sell each off at a prime price. Then you dispose of what you can't sell. All the organs go quickly when they're from the universal donor."

"But he's type A?"

"Which means the recipient needs to be type A or AB. If not, the organ would fail."

"Leaving the person right back where they started."

"With a much lighter bank account balance, if they weren't killed by the rejection first."

"Traceable?"

"Checking with local hospitals for transplant surgeries would help, but I don't know if it would help you. These hospitals get a good amount of money for the services. You think they would jeopardize all that with a bad reputation?"

"In other words, unless we get lucky, we have nothing. I'll have the captain put the word out to the local hospitals. Maybe something will break."

Victor takes a big bite out of his chocolate bar. I shake my head as he moans in pleasure at the offending candy. I miss bad food. Damn diets, ignoring carbohydrates, cookies, basically anything that tastes good. Frankie and her healthy dinners.

"Stop staring at my chocolate. You are more than capable of buying your own."

"You have any more?"

"No, did you not hear me about the divorce . . . my ex trying to take me for everything? I can barely afford these two immensely pleasurable treats. So, go upstairs. Talk to the captain and get the hell away from my chocolate."

He waves his hand in my face, but my eyes can only focus on the chocolate. Like a dog staring at a bone, I force myself to back away. Man, how I miss chocolate. It's one of those things that you don't necessarily think about or want until you see someone else eating it. The power of suggestion is just as bad as being on a diet. Either way, it sucks for me.

Chapter Six

E ver have those moments when you're the butt of a very cruel karmic joke? When you're walking and slip on nothing? Or you think you're at the top of the stairs but you're not, so that last giant step makes you look like a fool? I must be having one of those moments, because I keep pushing on this damn door and it's not budging.

"Need some help?" Logan says as I jump away from the door.

"It must be locked or something."

He smiles as he pulls the door open with ease. He holds it open as I enter the domain of uncertainty. Where everything I touch could be a bomb. Okay, maybe not a bomb, but I could delete an entire case file with a flick of my finger across the wrong monitor. It could happen. Trust me. Logan waves his hand, and I assume that means I am supposed to follow him to his office. Looking at the other minions as they stare at screens and click away, I realize my karmic smackdown has gone unnoticed.

Following Logan into his office, he closes the door behind me and looks rather intense.

"I assume you're here for the laptop we found at Mr. Miller's house?" Sitting on his desk, he places his hands on the computer in question.

"Just curious if you found anything."

"We found a lot of interesting information."

Sitting down in the same chair I had gotten comfortable in during my last visit, I rub my eyes and take a few breaths.

"You okay, detective?"

"No, just preparing myself for the migraine the information you are about to drop on me causes." He laughs at my comment. I wonder if he knows I'm serious. This much information for a computer illiterate individual is like trying to explain an atom bomb explosion to a newborn. The bomb goes off, but they do nothing but drool. I'm the newborn.

"It won't be that bad, I promise you. I'll try to—"

"Talk to me like a five-year-old?"

"Explain it better," he clarifies. I prefer my self-deprecating humor.

"Okay, hit me." Bold choice of words considering the situation.

"The computer had encrypted files all over the place. It took some time, but our team broke the code." He clicks a few buttons on the laptop and turns it to face me, revealing a live feed of the girls' locker rooms, bathrooms, and hallways.

"He rigged the whole house with cameras. We figured that out when we found his stash in the basement."

"Yes, but what you are looking at is live video streaming. He has cameras in the hallway to ensure that if he saw he was caught or in trouble, he could plan his escape route depending on where they were."

"Okay, sick fuck had video cameras watched women and young girls and made sure he could see where people were in case he needed to run. Got it."

"He also had access to this remotely."

"He could watch this anywhere?"

"Yes, there was a specific mobile access code embedded."

"Can a high school principal design and code something like this?"

"After looking over the profile and his past history, I don't think he knew how to do that. The thing is, the coding for this type of program is very innocuous on its own. You have to use it in a criminal way. So, legally speaking, the coding company did nothing wrong."

"That doesn't mean they didn't know what it was being used for."

"No, but it means they are protected under the law. It's like gun laws. The manufacturer makes the guns, but a person has to load and shoot it."

"Do we have a company?"

"Bridge the Gap, LLC. Owned and operated by Harry Brandt."

I nod at Logan. This is where my detective work takes over and he gets to sit and watch me work. Unless this Harry guy talks all technobabble. Then I'll be right back here begging Logan for a techie-to-Jasmine translator. I get up from the chair and stretch my joints. There's something about preparing for the worst that actually brings out the worst in your bones. Or I am old. I prefer it to be the former.

"Before you leave, we found that program Kaley had on her computer on Mr. Miller's as well. He saved his password, so we accessed his account. He had been in touch with D.B.M."

"Acronyms, the new nuisance of the digital world."

"Actually, they have been used for many years . . ."

"I get it. I was being a sarcastic bitch. It's what I do when I don't get something."

"Oh, sorry. Mr. Miller hired this individual to kill Mrs. Johnson and her son quietly. He was to torture and kill the father before bringing Kaley to Mr. Miller."

"Okay, so we had that idea already from the evidence. What makes this different?"

"According to the correspondence, Mr. Miller was supposed to help Kaley get away from the family. He was not supposed to keep her. He broke the contract. Payment or not, that is a huge no-no."

"Wait, if Miller wanted Kaley, why kill the son?"

"According to this, the boy was too young and not sellable."

"Kaley would never have agreed to that."

"If she was drugged, she had no concept of what she was doing."

"What would happen if you broke this kind of contract?"

"These kinds of people take their contracts very seriously. Imagine the mob when you don't pay. The worst part is you will never see them coming."

"They're everyday people hiding behind computer screens."

"Exactly. Not everyone is a nerd playing *World of Warcraft*."

"Thanks, Logan."

I head to the door and take another look at Hadley's movie poster.

"Hadley's at the convention center today. She should be signing autographs from four to about six tonight. You should stop by."

"Thanks, maybe I will."

Leaving the room, I swear I can hear the heads all swoosh back around to face their computer screens. They might be inhuman with their abilities, but curiosity can kill the cat. Staring the crowd down, I shake my head and laugh at myself. I am afraid of kids behind some flat piece of metal and plastic. What is the world coming to when these kids have my entire life at their fingertips? Why do I feel like I've discussed this before? Probably because I have. One way or another, I have wholeheartedly decided Chase is never getting a phone or a computer.

***

I pull up to the front of the obscene building in the middle of the city and park in the loading zone. I look over at the security guard as he begins to waddle toward to me. I love these rent-a-cops. They act like they have all the power in the world, but compared to my badge, they have nothing. In this case, my phallic symbol is bigger than his. I laugh to myself as the guard knocks on the hood of my truck. Okay, you can tap on the glass, wait for me to get out, but touch my family, my car, or my game room stuff—it's a step too far. I crack my neck, prepare for confrontation, and hop out of the car like a boxer ready for a fight.

"You can't park here."

"Maybe not, but I have the park anywhere in the city pass. So, I am."

I flash my badge and try to pass the man, but he holds his hand up. I can see he wants to push me back, show his manly dominance, but he's holding back.

"I'm here on official police business. You want to tell my captain that you denied me access to information on the murder and rape of a young girl? I would appreciate it if you let me go inside. Otherwise, you will force me to look for parking and waste precious time."

"Or you could follow the law you swore to uphold and move your car."

"Sir, I'm sorry for my partner here. We just want to go in and talk to a few people. We won't be long, so it shouldn't be that much of an issue."

I look at Will, and if my eyes could burn him, they would. He gently handles the security guard while I stew. I dislike when someone comes in and tries to save the day. Well, usually. When it saves my life, by all means try your best to intervene.

"Not too long."

Will grabs my elbow and pulls me toward the high-rise's doors.

"And keep her away from me!"

The doors open automatically, and I pull against Will hard. I have a short fuse. Like really short when it comes to stupidity, especially people who think they are real officers of the law or know the law better than I do. No matter how hard I try, I can't seem to break Will's grasp. Before I know it, I'm pulled into an elevator, and Will's hitting the button to move the tin can up.

"Let it go."

"Why the hell do people think because they have a toy store badge they're a real cop?"

"You were parking illegally."

"I have the city pass."

"Doesn't mean you should abuse it."

"Investigating a crime is not an abuse. You saw how bad parking was."

"Well, yes, but you could have used the pass two blocks down, like I did."

"That was so far away though." I pout.

The door opens, and walking out, I notice the full wall of windows. It offers a stunning view of the city, or your death if you fall. You can feel the building sway as it creaks. I hate being up this high. Looking around the area, my eyes land on several vertical cracks along the wall.

"Blame the latest hurricane." The receptionist looks at me. The block on the counter says Kiernan Jones. Interesting name for a girl.

"Fixing it soon I hope?"

"That was three years ago. Nothing gets fixed if it costs money." She stands up and walks toward the main doors. Pulling them open, she waves someone over. I reach into my pocket, but Kiernan stops me with her perfectly manicured nails.

"We know who you are, detectives. We've been made aware of the situation. Mr. Brandt thought you would be here sooner, but better late than never."

"Thank you, Kiernan," I mutter as I walk past her.

She nods, walks back to her desk, and sits down, her attention no longer on me but on her cell phone social media profile. I bet she has enough information online to give away her identity and have a stalker. What you don't know won't hurt you . . . I guess. Until you're on Victor's table. Then it did.

The intern struggles against the weight of a heavy glass door. Holding it open for Will and me to walk in, he fights to close the door silently, his thin arms struggling to hold it. Beads of sweat form on his forehead as he ensures the closure is complete. Looking up to me, his eyes widen and he rushes away.

"Detective Everts, Detective Steele, how can I help you today?"

Harry Brandt stands to his full height of holy crap and taller than the six-foot Marine next to me. I'd say he was six feet three or five inches. Not to mention, his muscles stretch his shirt to the ripping point. He's not wrestler huge, but you can see every cut. His perfectly trimmed beard, manicured nails, and styled hair screams to me of a man who needs to be in control. He waves his uncalloused hands to the chairs in front of his desk.

"Please, have a seat."

Will shakes Harry's hand and then sits down calmly. I'm too busy walking around looking at the frames with various pictures in them.

"We're just here regarding some information about a program developed here. It was used in accessing the dark web. Two individuals were later found dead."

"That's terrible, but what does this have to do with me and my company?"

"We were hoping there was a list of purchases, clients who have used it? Maybe you were hacked and the program was stolen?"

"We develop many programs here; I truthfully can't say for sure until I know what we're looking for."

Will reaches into his jacket pocket and pulls out a small flash drive, handing it to Harry. The larger man plugs it into his laptop, and I can hear the drive booting up. The view is more stunning in his office. I wonder if the glass is body proof. I'm sure it would take a couple of hits, but eventually even epoxy has to give. Then it's a one-way trip to hell. People who hurt children deserve to be there.

"This is something we developed a long time ago."

"Does it have a name?" I ask. This way I can call it something other than "the program." That sounds too much like an eighties' movie title.

"The wonders of an open-source program is that it can be anything you want it to be. All it takes is a download and a dream." He smirks at me, and I see Will's shoulders tense. Even he's getting the sleazy vibe off this guy. I'm sure this type of guy has been around forever, from mobsters to modern-day hackers. Narcissism doesn't die just as technology changes. My phone beeps. Unlocking it, I read a text from Logan and my blood pressure begins to rise.

"How did you find the funding to start this venture?"

"I don't see how that's relevant, detective."

"Irving Garrison helped develop this building and, according to our sources, bankrolled your venture here."

"Be that as it may, I still fail to see what this has to do with some open-source, free-to-the-public code."

"My techs would like a list of IP addresses that accessed and down-loaded the program in question." Will changes the direction of the conversation. His tone tells me he's irritated I brought up Garrison again. I wish I could say I blame him, but I don't.

"While I would love to help with your investigation, I'm sure you understand I can't just hand that over."

"We could get a warrant." I toss in my normal worded message. He will, of course, respond by telling me to go get it.

"I would appreciate that, detective. Thank you."

I watch him stand and walk to the door, basically telling us to get the hell out.

Following Will to the door, I stop in front of Mr. Brandt. "See you soon."

"I doubt it, Jasmine. How is Frankie doing? I saw that Chase is doing well on our latest game release. Maybe he and I will play sometime."

He smiles at me again, and this time I feel a chill roll down my spine. I do my best not to let it show, but he knows he got to me. My mind moves a hundred miles a minute as I ponder the veiled threat. Chase is online playing all the time, but who is he really playing the game with? I doubt I could ever get him to stop playing it. Even if I get the names of the kids he plays with, a good hacker can impersonate that player seamlessly.

I walk into the elevator next to a slightly irritated Detective Everts.

"You have a reason for bringing Garrison in this?"

Mindlessly opening my phone, I show him the text from Logan. He calms down and nods at the new information.

"You okay?"

"Yeah," I lie. "I'm going to go to the convention center and see Hadley."

"Finally going to talk to her?"

The elevator doors open, and I just walk away. Sometimes, you just can't say anything when your mind is full of everything.

***

There are few places on this planet where you feel you are not part of this world. The oceans, anytime there are bunches of kiddies running around, and at any comic book or science fiction convention. I purchase a general admission ticket and gag at the price. Thank the powers that be for credit cards. Or just thank greed and corporate America, your choice. The skinny, volunteer, barely-out-of-diapers kid scans my pass, and I walk into that other world.

You name the character from your favorite show, and I promise you there is someone here in costume. I'm not looking for them though. As I weave through the rows of tables and swarms of fans, my eyes flick from the map and to the markings around the hall. This place needs GPS.

"Detective Steele, you're here!"

I turn to see Logan with a bottle of water in his hand and a coffee in the other.

"Thought I would see if Hadley was here."

"Oh sure, she's in the back. Follow me."

Logan walks through the crowd, and I get to see the back of his shirt, which features Hadley's face, blood dripping out of her mouth, vampire teeth pressing into her lower lip. The image causes my breath to hitch a bit. Not because of the teeth, but the blood. I swallow my irrational thoughts as Logan walks up to a table and places the bottle of water on it. He stands back and there is Hadley, her hair darker than the time I last saw her, laughing with the fan in front of her. Logan leans down and whispers something in her ear. She looks up and finds me in the crowd. The emotions that one feels when facing their past, their fears, and their regrets . . . it's impossible to describe. There are no words.

Hadley says something to the line of people in front of her table as she turns back to face me. I watch her take a few steps toward me before security stops her. My feet, as they sometimes do, walk on their own accord until I am right in front of the security guard.

"She's with me," Hadley tells the men, and he moves the barrier, letting me inside the safety zone.

"Hey, Had, I'm—" Before I can finish my thought, her arms are around my neck, and she pulls me in for a hug.

"Doesn't matter."

Leaning down, I admit I relish the hug from my friend. I've missed her witty comebacks, her innocent comments, just everything. Like all real family, blood and time seem to matter little. Pulling back, she grabs my hand and leads me to her table. She calmly wipes the few stray tears that fell from her eyes and sits down.

"Stay. I'll be done in a while and we can sit in the back for a bit. I see you met Logan already. I'm sure you two have lots in common. He works for the police department too!"

I can see Hadley my friend disappear and Hadley the actress pops up. Her smile is larger, her eyes more engaging. She's on for the paying public. It's a true talent. Logan pulls back the curtain and motions for me to follow him. Finding a nice set of folding chairs and tables, we sit down.

"You know Hadley?"

"Yeah, I do." I watch him fumble with his coffee cup, spinning it within his fingers. His eyes fixate on them, as if unable to focus on anything else. His leg slowly bounces as his body fills with nerves. It doesn't take a detective to know; this is why he let me know where she was.

"You're dating her."

His eyes pop up and lock with mine.

"Doesn't take a genius to figure it out. How long?"

"About a year."

A year. That's while I was still healing from my injuries. When I was hiding from the world and all its drama. When I couldn't bear to see her in pain. When I abandoned her as a friend. He was there. I didn't know. I'm both envious of him and angry at myself.

"How did you meet?"

"I was investigating someone hacking a local hospital's wireless system. There were fears of changing the frequencies of pacemakers and other things. Anyway, she happened to be there for physical therapy. After seeing her there more than once, I decided to bring her coffee. She started talking to me, and it turned into a routine."

"You bringing her coffee during therapy?"

"Yes."

"Thank you."

"Jasmine, there's nothing to thank me for."

I shrug my shoulders and ignore his comment. He might have done it for himself, but he inadvertently made me feel better about the situation.

"Can we talk shop for a minute before Hadley comes back here?"

"Sure, hit me with your best shot, Logan."

"I found the profile for D.B.M. I sent him a message about a job. Now we just wait and see."

"You did what?" My voice cracks with slight anger considering what he just told me about his relationship with my friend.

"It was cleared with the captain. I contacted him; now we wait for him to respond."

"And if he doesn't?"

"Then I wasted my personal time sending an email."

"You said these type of people were good. They do research, they pay attention and make sure they are comfortable before accepting a deal. So, what the hell makes you think he isn't doing this now?"

"I made a calculated risk assessment and felt it was worth it."

"Here I am thanking you for helping Hadley when I couldn't, and you go right around and do the same damn thing I did to her."

"I did nothing to her."

"Logan, you've put her in harm's way again!"

"Mind telling me why you two are causing a scene out here?"

We both turn and see an annoyed Hadley standing, arms folded, shaking her head. She walks over to our small table and sits down next to Logan. Her eyes flash from him to me, waiting for an answer.

"I'm sorry, baby. Jasmine and I are working a case together. We were just talking shop, and I know how much you hate hearing about all that stuff."

"Jazz? You have something to add to this conversation?"

Her eyes bore into my head. She wants me to answer, but I know if I say something, it won't help. As she waits patiently, I search my mind for something to say that won't involve me lying. My phone rings in my pocket, effectively cutting off all thoughts.

"Steele."

I look at the two in front of me. Logan looks nervous while Hadley just stares blankly. I think she knows I am about to walk away again.

"I'll be right there."

"You have to go already?"

"I'm sorry, Had. I promise it won't be for long this time."

"About the case?"

"Yes, but we'll talk another time. Just please look into the man funding everything. That is what I need you to do."

Logan nods as I stand up to leave. Hadley walks me to the edge of her autograph section. After I give her a quick hug, she watches me leave the wide-open space of her celebrity to the swarm of cattle moving from table to table. Even though I hate crowds, this was a good thing to do.

***

The doors of the elevator open on the fifth floor of the hospital, revealing a few uniformed officers, a woman crying into a nurse's arms, and the captain standing in a corner rubbing his temples. This doesn't look good.

"Good, you're here."

Will walks up to me, pen and pad in his hand.

"What's going on?"

Will motions down the hallway, and like a perfectly trained puppy, I follow. If I ever get put in a hospital again, this is the place to be. There are more doctors on this floor than the rest of the place, I bet. Well, fewer nurses, and frankly they're more valuable. It's neither here nor there, I guess.

"Jake Morris, on the transplant list for a liver." He stops and turns to face me.

"So, what's the time of death?"

"I'm not dead yet, detective. Soon, but not yet."

That's when I see Mr. Morris, alive and well but handcuffed to the hospital bed.

"Rejection?"

I walk into the room and stare at the man as if he's an oddity in the world. Hell, he is. I'm a homicide detective. I don't get to see live victims. It's always the family members and their losses. I want to poke him to make sure he's real, but that's childish.

I do it anyway.

"Ow!"

"Sorry, just checking."

"I assure you, detective, I am still living and breathing."

"What happened?"

"I'm in liver failure."

"Right, the metal on your wrist is decoration only."

"We just need to hear your side of the story," Will throws in to bring the conversation back to the point at hand.

"Look, I know this sucks, and you must be livid at your situation, but we need to know who did this to you." I find myself feeling compassion for this guy. He must have been so desperate to resort to buying organs online. That couldn't have been an easy conversation with his family. If he had one.

"My son's only seven. I just wanted a chance to see him grow up."

I understand that more than my words could ever express. My brother and his wife would have given anything for ten more minutes with Chase.

"I was reading some forums online, downloaded a program, and found a listing for various organs."

"You were on the transplant list. The sicker you are, the more likely you are—"

"I'm an alcoholic. Would you donate part of your liver to me?"

My silence speaks volumes.

"Neither would I. Apparently, when you've already had a donation and screw it up, they don't like you very much. I had no choice. Seriously, detective, what would you do?"

Stop drinking and put my family first?

"It doesn't matter what I would have done. You chose the path you did, and now you are going to pay the price for it."

"I just don't get it. He was listed as type O, a universal donor. I paid a shitload of money for a small section of liver. It was supposed to regenerate and make me a healthy man. They lied."

I want to smack this man. He lied to his family. He chose to continue to drink and put them at risk. He chose these things, and now doesn't want to deal with the ramifications. When the hell will people learn you reap what you sow?

Turning on my heels, I walk out of the room. I head over to Victor, who is in deep conversation with the captain.

"The DNA matches Mr. Miller. It's definitely from his body."

"So, that's why I was called."

"Steele, that might be the primary reason, but there is more to it. The district attorney is hesitant a judge will issue a warrant."

"That information is vital to our case."

Victor watches the two of us talking, his head bouncing back and forth.

"Victor, how long does Mr. Morris have?"

"If he responds to the medication, it is possible to bypass rejection, or it will completely fail and die. Truthfully, there is no timetable here."

"He's convinced he's going to die."

"I know. Hopefully, it gives him time to think about life decisions."

He smiles as he walks away from the captain and me. Turning my attention back to Tyler, I can see these last few cases have aged him greatly. Being a captain, dealing with the red tape and bureaucracy can't be easy on him.

"You want to tell me why the DA isn't sure we have enough to go for a warrant?"

"He feels we need something more solid before going after a computer company that employs a large number of people. Not to mention he has a wonderful history of giving back to the community."

"Two dead bodies, two laptops, and a program connecting it all to a company isn't enough?"

"Not in an election year, apparently." He runs his hand through what's left of the hair on his head. "I need you to be careful with this case. Mr. Pevy let me know that Irving Garrison was behind the company's startup capital. I don't need to worry about you here, do I?"

"I promise you I'll follow the evidence wherever it leads. If it leads to his doorstep, I will hit him square between the eyes." I turn away and head back to the elevator. Pushing the button a little harder than I needed to, I try to hide my frustration with the people around me.

"Steele, this isn't just about you. Remember that."

I search the captain's eyes for understanding but find none. He's questioning my ability; I don't like it. This isn't like last time. This isn't the same thing. This is me trying to do the best I can do with the evidence I have. The world closes in on me, and my breath catches in my throat. No matter what I do, no matter how hard I work, it's never going to be enough.

Chapter Seven

S ometimes when you stare at something long enough, the words or images on the page begin to move. My eye doctor told me it had to do with dryness, some retina thing, or like a reflection. I don't remember; he just said it was my natural eye doing its best to drive me nuts. My mother, on the other hand, called it "an excuse to get out of school to go to the doctor-itis."

Staring at the case files in front of me, I feel that same sensation when the words begin to move. Mom would be smacking me in the back of the head. She might tell me to focus on one thing and don't stare at it like a panting dog. Yeah, her analogies were usually odd, but what do you expect from your mother? I lean back, rubbing my eyes, smiling because I know I am more like my mother every day. Not such a bad thing.

This case is a bad thing. It reeks of stupidity, greed, and more stupidity. If people were smarter, kinder, and showed a bit more compassion, then half of the crimes I deal with would be gone. There wouldn't be votes against civil liberties, no shooting children over clothing, and less murder. Who am I kidding? This is reality, and people will always take the easy route instead of the hard-working one. Where there is a will, there is a lawsuit or someone on the dark web willing to sell it to you. The world is a selfie-obsessed, narcissistic society, and I am raising a child in it. My mother never had to deal with this shit.

"I brought you some coffee."

Frankie walks into the bedroom and hands me a steaming mug of heavenly goodness. She always knows when I need a break or a pick-me-up. Lately, it's been more of a way to start conversations. I'm not avoiding her per se. I'm working hard to figure out how to answer her questions. I keep going back to that damn fork in the road. Do I walk left and rehash the same pain or pick a new path that I don't know? Why can't this be easy?

"Thanks," I mumble as I feel the warmth travel down my throat into my stomach.

Frankie collects the loose pages of the file and puts them neatly to the side. She sits down, and I know a serious conversation is coming soon.

"Can we talk?"

"Sure." Mental note: do not roll eyes. Do not disrespect whatever it is she is going to say. Do not, under any circumstances, laugh at her. I can utter those words regularly, but I feel my brain never gets the memo.

"You keep avoiding me."

"It's a difficult case."

"You also forget who you're talking to. This case hasn't been easy on me either."

"I'm sorry." Leave it to me to forget that Kaley was her patient. One she could have saved, but the law and a mother prevented her from helping.

"I feel I could have done more. It was my job to do more."

"You can't think like that, Frankie. We both know you went out of your way to protect Kaley. Her mother prevented it from happening. Her mother, Frankie, not you. Will and I scoured your files, and there was nothing in there that made either of us feel you let her down. You know I'm biased as hell, but Will would call you out."

"Yes, I guess he would."

"I know this is going to eat you up for a long time. Trust me, I know that. Maybe you should talk to someone to help you deal with this?"

"A shrink for a shrink?"

"I always wondered if you guys shared each other as patients."

"Shared each other?"

"You know, like psycho babbled each other as patients, not colleagues."

"You're an ass."

"Yes, but you love me."

Kissing Frankie has got to be the best addiction I've ever had. Look, sex is great; it's amazing even, but it's nothing like kissing her. There could be any emotion packed into a kiss, and it's freely given to me. I swear it tells me she loves me without saying a word. Or without having to quickly get dressed because the kid will be up and demanding breakfast in a few hours.

Pulling away from my lips, she smiles at me and takes a calming breath. Sometimes a kiss can do that too.

"Will called while you were sleeping. The gang should be here soon to go over the case like old times."

My mother always felt when you found your true love, you would know it. I knew it the moment I laid eyes on Frankie. I wanted the house, the picket fence, the two-point-five kids, and a two-car garage. Or a mansion in the Hollywood Hills. I'm not picky. But . . .

"I always wanted to have more than one kid." I smack myself in the face, covering my mouth. What the hell did I just say out loud? Looking up, I see Frankie staring at me wide-eyed, dumbfounded.

"You what?" She looks innocent, but she wants me to repeat what I said. I know it. It's a way to prove I wasn't an ass and actually said what

I really meant to say. Damn Freudian slip. Removing my hand, I have to face the music, storm, ramifications, and all of what I just said.

"I've always seen us with more than one kid. Just not our own."

"Okay, I don't follow."

"I have no desire to give birth. I mean seriously, I have absolutely no desire to deal with watermelon-sized things with an escape route the size of a pea. I just can't."

"Your mother—"

"STOP!" My hands slam over my ears like a five-year-old hearing how they were brought into this world. Who am I kidding? I'm still five in a lot of ways. Frankie pulls my hands away and sits back down on the bed.

"I'm sorry. I forgot how you feel about that."

"The stork is real. That is all."

"Yes, dear. You were saying?"

"We have so many obstacles facing us. People passing legal discrimina-tion laws, certain states allowed to re-educate us . . . hell, some want it to be a criminal offense punishable by law. I don't want to bring a newborn into that. They wouldn't have asked for this."

"So, we adopt a child and put them into this horrible life we have?" The sarcasm is dripping from her words, and I know I am on thin ice.

"No. Well, yes, but not like that. We have all this crap swarming around us in general, but we also have so much love to give a child, you know? These kids have no one to help them. They're alone without anyone to truly call on for anything. Maybe we can bring someone who has nothing and offer them a little bit of crazy."

"A little bit of crazy, huh?"

"Depending on if Xbox is involved, then it's a lot crazy."

"You two and your games." Her lips meet mine, and I'm reminded once again how amazing this woman is. I wonder if my mother would mind me living in sin or scream at me to marry Frankie. Interesting how I could reasonably agree to adopting a kid, but marriage freaks me out. Maybe because I know adoption can take years.

"You head downstairs. I'll be there in a minute for more coffee." Grab-bing the file folder, I flip through it, making sure the contents are still in the proper order.

"I love you," Frankie whispers before moving out into the hallway. I'm going to marry that woman . . . someday.

***

There is a comfort one finds in friendly chaos. It's something we have no control over, yet we seem to embrace it. We willingly watch the orchestral movements as if there was some maestro waving their hands to and fro. Maybe we all subconsciously do it, but the end result is the same. A beautiful ballet of crazy.

Will's wrangling the whiteboard into the room, while Chase sits on the couch, bored. Frankie flips through a file folder on the table. Must be one of Kaley's. Victor is animatedly waving his hands all about trying to communicate with Will. My Marine partner, on the other hand, looks like he's disarming a weapon of mass destruction as he tries to get the board not to flip. Reminds me of Christmas morning when Chase was little. He would carry everything over to the wrong person and start to open it. Sometimes he'd tell you what it was. "Here you go, Frankie; it's a wallet." I think that should be the definition of family. It's not about blood distinctions or choice; it's those who create a chaos we feel comfortable in. Family equals total, unequivocal chaos.

"You agree with me, don't you, Jazz?"

"What?" I mumble before taking another long sip of the delicious liquid.

"Victor, she's only on cup number one." Frankie smiles at me, giving me an excuse to hide in my thoughts for a bit longer. After our conversation upstairs, I wasn't sure how she would react around our friends. She knows how I feel about keeping things quiet until they are true, happening, and physically cannot be taken away. We've been through so much together; I don't want either of us to feel that loss again. You can get your hopes up, tell the world and enjoy the excitement, then feel the pity when it doesn't happen. So, we err on the side of caution. No matter what it is, from Chase wanting to switch sports to adoption, we stay quiet.

"Sheesh, it's like you people allow anyone to come here!"

Victor breaks my reverie with his words. He wraps his arms around Hadley as she hesitantly walks into the room. Frankie and Will follow suit before Chase jumps off the couch and rams his not so little body into her, his face hidden as she kisses his head. Chase nods his head at something Hadley says. She hands him something, and he runs off to his room. It has to be something for his Xbox, probably from Logan, but who cares as long as the kid is happy. Unless it's porn; then I won't be happy. Seriously, I am more like my mother every day.

"You going to sit there and stare into space or are you going to say hello?"

Standing, I give Hadley a hug and drop my head on her shoulder. As I loosen my grip on her, I feel her pull me tighter. It's a simple gesture; she needs the hug as much as I do. Maybe it's her way of healing, making sure I'm real. Survivor's guilt can and does suck.

"Hope you don't mind me coming by. Vic called and told me about the crime powwow. Thought . . ."

"Of course, why would you think—?" I stop talking as I see her face fall. I've been avoiding her until recently; why else would she feel this way.?

"Ladies, can we get started?"

Hadley finds a space on the couch, and I feel a game of Pictionary coming on. Will pulls out a picture of Harry Brandt and sticks it to the whiteboard with a magnet. Pulling out the black marker, he scribbles some things under the picture.

"Okay, so far we have Harry Brandt, possible suspect. Being a bit of a hard-ass, so it's hard to get a read on where we stand with him."

"The software used to access the deep web . . ."

"Dark web," Hadley corrects me. I wave my hand and give her the floor. She's dating the man, so he would of course fill her in on the details.

"The program is open-source; anyone can download it at any time and make various changes. What he's not saying is that the program itself was designed to be the gateway to the unknown space. It was up to the other coding people to change things to suit their needs."

"Might help us get a warrant."

"There's no way to prove intent in the coding. He could simply say he designed it to search the entire web; the usage was unintentional."

"Logan is really rubbing off on you," I say proudly. She looks lighter, happier, free of the drama.

"Who's Logan?" Victor pipes up, and Hadley's face drops with a mix of fear and trepidation.

"He's the tech guy; huge Hadley Moreno fan. Didn't he come by the convention the other day?"

Hadley turns to look at me with a slight smile on her face. It's the one that says thanks, but it isn't necessary.

"Yes, he did. He should be here to fill in the gaps with all this technology stuff. I only know what we discuss over dinner."

"You should have brought him," Frankie casually tosses out. There's a feeling where you are part of something, but you have no concept of what's really going on. I've got that right now. It seems like I am missing something.

"We have enough coffee to go around. Why don't you give him a call?"

They all know who he is. They aren't asking anything about how they met, who he is, or whatever else friends would normally grill about. They all knew. It's an odd sensation, knowing your friends all kept something from you. Sure, there are extenuating circumstances, but seriously, right now I don't care. It hurts. No matter how much you grow as an adult, you can still be easily hurt by those you love. Either you deal with it, or you hide it deep inside and let it fester.

"So, going back to the program?" Or you ignore it and move on. Effectively, I let things fester. Good old reliable ignoring the problem with the hopes that it will go away on its own. Like Chase's smelly gas explosions. You just pinch your nose and walk away.

"Brandt had to know what it would be used for, but there's no way to prove his intent."

"True, but it might be enough to get us a warrant for the IP addresses. Then we go from there." Will writes on the board as he speaks.

"That's all well and good, but how does Kaley fall into all of this?"

"She decided her only option to end the abuse was via murder for hire," Victor calmly states as he props his feet on my couch. My brother's nice couch, to be exact. Just as the anger bubbles and I feel the words on my lips, Frankie pushes his feet off the couch.

"If you stay here, feet off the furniture," she says as she sits down next to him, blocking the return of Victor's feet.

Victor closes the marker and cracks his neck as he walks away from the board.

"Basically, we have everything tied up in who got the program and who they contacted."

"If the IP addresses help us at all. Who's to say the people who downloaded it are the actual people using it. These people are kings of anonymity," I say as I stand and move to the board.

"It might lead us to who this guy is, but there's no trail in CODIS. No DNA in the system. Even if we could find out who did this, we could only connect him to it by emails."

"Which are time and date stamped," Hadley defends her position.

"All it takes is a defense attorney capable of putting people on the jury who either hate the internet, hate the government following our searches, or are kids who feel once it's deleted, it's gone." Frankie rubs her eyes in frustration.

"So, I'll go over the bodies again and dig for more," Victor tosses out. I love it when people try to prove points and defend their positions. They offer up more work, yet in my mind, you technically should have done that in the first place. Considering how anal-retentive Victor is, I know there is nothing more for those bodies to tell.

"Well, if the information turns out to be a dead end, then Brandt might be your only suspect." Hadley leans back on the couch, sending a text to Logan, I assume.

"Had, I appreciate that, but there's no forensic evidence to link him to it."

"You've gotten a DA to indict on circumstantial evidence before."

"She's right, Jasmine. This is a solid lead on Mr. Brandt. He could be the man in question. Physically, he easily fits the profile. Mentally, he is very close to it."

"But he doesn't fit it financially, Frankie. He needed help."

Picking up the marker, I start to write Irving Garrison's name on the board. I hear Will grumble in the background, but I really don't care. This is right in front of their faces, and they are choosing to ignore it.

"What does he have to do with this?"

"Had, it's all about the money. If you follow the money, we have a perfect triangle of cause. Garrison funds Brandt's office and has him develop the dark web access coding. Miller asks his childhood friend Garrison to give him access. After that, Miller contacts D.B.M. to kill the family, so he can have Kaley for himself. It all connects."

"Theoretically, but not in a factual sense. It might be logical, but why would he want the code? Why would he allow everyone to have access? How would it benefit him? Irving Garrison is not a giving man, so this seems all out of character."

I see Frankie's eyes, begging me to forgive her for speaking up. That feeling of betrayal creeps up, especially knowing that I was the last to be aware of Hadley's relationship. It's hard to let that go, but as an adult I'm expected to.

"Will, let's go see if the district attorney will get us a warrant for Bridge the Gap customer listings."

Without saying another word, I grab what I need and leave the room. Sometimes it is better to say nothing than to try and defend yourself. If this was any other person, I guarantee you no one in that room would be saying anything about connections. Yet, because it's the father of the fool who shot me, I'm obsessing. Maybe I am, but it's not anyone. Why is it when you want support, you face criticism, but when you don't need support, everyone wants to help you?

***

Will was quiet the entire ride over, and I'm thankful for it. I don't need him being rational or telling me how they are only looking out for my best interest. Right now, I don't care. Standing in the elevator, I shoot Logan a quick text. At least it feels like *someone* is on my side. If nothing else, the information he might find can prove me wrong. Either way, he's not giving me an outright no. Could be because of who he's dating and he's trying to make a positive impression on me, but I'll take what I can get.

"Detectives, Mr. Brandt was expecting you." Kiernan stares at her phone as she speaks. I really want to take that phone and smash it. She reminds me of the kind of person who would break into your house but sue you when they get hurt smashing a window to leave.

"Mind explaining to me how he always knows we're coming?"

"You're the detective; it's not my fault you all use antiquated methods." She smiles as she goes back to her phone. At this point, I really wonder what she could really accomplish on the small-ass device.

"Yes, well, real detective work takes time." My patience is slowly slipping away.

"Right, keep telling yourself that. You remember where it is, right? Cool." She continues to move her thumbs over the screen. Instead of putting criminals in prisons, we should take away their cell phones, computers, and gaming systems. Make these nonviolent criminals do community service with a group home and make it a violation of parole to have anything connected to the internet. That is definitely a great tactic, and it would save taxpayers millions. I should run for office or design rides at Disney. It's kind of the same thing; you control the masses one way or another.

Will walks ahead of me through the maze of desks to Brandt's office. If you pay attention, you can see the slight glances and some glares he gets. Some want to stare at his ass, others want to knock him on it. Human beings' obscure reactions amuse me greatly. I wonder if half of these people can hold a conversation outside of instant or text messages. This is the technology generation; they code an android to do it for them.

Will stops in front of Brandt's office and stares at me. I know the look. He's silently telling me not to bring up Garrison. I nod in understanding, but I also know I'll do whatever the case needs. If that leads to connections and questions about his funding, so be it. Walking inside, the two of us take our seats. I'll let Will take the lead on this one. No one wants my opinion right now anyway. Can't have my gut getting in the way.

"Mr. Brandt, we appreciate you speaking with us again."

"Not like I had a choice, detective. It was either let you in or have you break down the doors. We have a company to run. Can't afford to have your men acting like bulls in a china shop."

"We have a warrant for those addresses."

He leans forward and grabs the piece of paper. His eyes scan the page, but the response we usually get when serving these is missing. He's distant, calm, less afraid of what we'll find. He's not sweating. He's not freaking. He hasn't pushed any buttons warning of incoming doom. He is simply reading.

"As you can see," Will continues, "it gives us access not only to the addresses where downloads were completed but also any personal information the customer entered in order to download the files in question."

"Yes, I see that. My question is why?"

"As we discussed prior, that information would allow us to pinpoint who used your program and when."

"Yes, but you understand that number is in the millions."

"We would just need those local to the tri-state area."

"Again, that could be in the millions. The proverbial needle in a haystack. Maybe you should focus on what you do have instead of trying to uncover what you don't. Isn't the rule to follow the evidence?"

He's right. We should be following the evidence, but in its absence, you have to look for said needle and pray.

"The evidence led us here, Mr. Brandt."

"Obviously. It also led you to try and trample on my rights of free enterprise."

I can see Will's right hand flex into a tight fist, his knuckles white. I might have to open my mouth to prevent him from breaking Mr. Brandt's.

"Maybe we are," I pipe up, and I can feel the heat of Will's glare on me. "Maybe we're not. We know you're connected. None of this shit really matters. One way or another, you created the program that was used in the commission of a crime. So, we'll just arrest you and let you rot in a cell for things you claim you had no control over."

He stares at me, and I know the look well. He feels he is better than me. It's not just his narcissism about his looks or his dominating height. Nope, this person is a full-on psycho with the idea that the world revolves around him. I love bringing these kinds of people back down to Earth. Kind of like the civil liberties argument. Some say my life is a sin; I simply say "I'll save you a seat in hell." Conversation over. Stupidity and this type of domineering behavior shouldn't be tolerated in today's day and age. Yet here I am in the office of said controlling person, and I am supposed to respect their idiocy. The older I get, the more I dislike what humanity has become.

"I have a team of lawyers that would eat those charges for breakfast."

"Maybe," I coolly state. "Then again, maybe not. You willing to take that chance?"

"I don't know, detective." He leans forward on his desk, dark eyes focused solely on me. "Are you?"

Will stands up, his hands balled into fists as he leans toward Brandt. I can't help but smile guiltily. I'm enjoying this standoff. It's kind of fun seeing what buttons I can push.

"If you would please get your hands off my client's desk," a woman says behind me. I was so focused on my enjoyment, I didn't hear the door open. Bad Jasmine.

"You would be?" Will hastily asks her, his frustration oozing with every word.

"Mr. Brandt's attorney."

"Excellent, we have a warrant. So you can make sure this individual here hands everything over to us. Then we'll be on our way," I tell her as I stand up and fix my shirt.

"No, you don't. Your warrant is a violation of several federal and state statutes. Therefore, Judge Killian quashed it this morning."

She pushes a folded piece of paper into my chest. She wants to play hardball. Okay, let's play. I take hold of her hand and squeeze tightly. Leaning in closely, my mouth inches away from her ear, I say, "We'll have the DA deal with this but know it isn't over."

Letting go of her hand, I brush past her, making my power known. I can hear Will grunt as he walks behind me. I have a feeling I am going to hear about this back at the precinct. Lord knows the woman is already on the phone with the DA's office filing a complaint. Granted, maybe I deserve it, but people would probably file one if I posted too many bacon photos to my Twitter account. If I had one, that is. It's not like I shot her while she was running away, and she assaulted me first. *Keep telling yourself that, Jasmine.*

***

Heading to work is always an annoying prospect. I either want to sleep in or be out on patrol. Anything to avoid doing paperwork, dealing with the office drama, or my boss. I blame my issues with Officer Garrison taking over my case and then trying to kill me. It doesn't feel safe like it used to. It's like when you decide to date your ex again. Trust must be built up again. You have to see if you actually work as a team or as individuals. It's the same thing with anything really. I have to see if I even want to be in this building. I want the job, but maybe this building isn't for me anymore.

The place is practically a ghost town, and I'm hoping the captain is off somewhere else. Will dropped me off to go deal with his kids. Something about checking up on their social media profiles. I think he's heading to the gym to blow off some steam first. He looked like he could punch a wall and rebuild it just to obliterate it again. I understand his pain.

"Detective Steele, a word in my office."

Shit. This is where the ability to choose our own path is nonexistent. I would love to take the path more traveled and run the hell out of the building. It's the safe route. The one that doesn't leave a disciplinary note in my file. It's also the one that could lead to me being fired. Alas, I will do what every other grunt who needs to make a living does and take it from the man in charge. Unless the lawyer chick didn't call; then this might be a normal conversation among colleagues.

Walking through the office door, I see two shot glasses and a bottle of Patron on the desk. Captain Udall waves at me, and I close the door with a loud, terrifying click. He points to the chair like a man picking out a good piece of steak. I sit and prepare to be roasted. He takes the seat next to me, in case he wants to choke me, I guess.

"I got a nice phone call this morning from the powers that be. You pissed in someone's coffee when you dealt with Brandt this morning."

I stay silent as he pours two shots and hands me one.

"As of right now, we're both off duty."

He tips his head back and drains his glass. He stares at me expectantly, and I don't hesitate in drinking up.

"Want to explain to me what happened?" Tyler says as he fills our glasses again.

"Captain, should we really be drinking here?"

"My office is like Vegas," he mutters. "Unless I'm on duty or some high-powered official is in here. Then it's an open book." He hands me my glass. I drain it quickly and slam it back on the desk.

"We showed up, and he wasted our time until some chick walks in with a signed injunction. Nothing more, nothing less."

"So, you didn't threaten this high-powered attorney with retribution?"

"What is it with these money people? Trust me, Cap, if I wanted to threaten her, she would have felt it."

"Jasmine, we all know your bark is worse than your bite. All I know is the powers that be informed me that you are to stay away from Mr. Brandt, his offices, and his lawyers until further notice."

"If I refuse?"

"You'll be arrested, and that wouldn't look very good for the creditability of the case. Not to mention Frankie would kill you."

"Is it bad I'm more afraid of her than jail?" I joke as I pour another shot for the two of us.

"No, I'm more afraid of my wife as well. Nature of the ring on my hand."

"I don't have one of those."

"No. You just keep that engagement ring in my home safe. You want it back?"

"Maybe. Eventually. Who the hell knows? I haven't seen it since the night Henry died."

"Then let me sell it and you'll get a new one."

"Tyler, that's the one she picked out. That's the one she'll get if I ever give it to her."

He leans back in the chair, sips the Patron, and gives me a onceover. I can see he's trying to figure out what to say next or how to phrase it. Watching his eyes, the way they dart around, and the way his forehead wrinkles and relaxes speaks volumes. "I don't want to talk about it." I cut his thoughts off to save my own sanity.

"Okay. Then let's talk about this case. Judge Killian signed the injunction."

"Yea, something about violating some statutes."

He takes another shot before closing the bottle. He stands, walks around his desk, and pulls open the bottom drawer. He's thinking, buying time to piece together his next words. He puts the bottle away, closes the drawer, and leans on the desk facing me.

"What does your gut say?"

"Someone wants this to go away quickly. I have my suspicions about connections, but nothing solid. The one thing I know for sure is that evidence doesn't lie. It's thin, misleading, and frankly a pain in the ass to find right now, but what we have points to Harry Brandt."

"As the killer?"

"Plausible, but he could also be protecting the perp. The judge had no right to block our warrant. We need to know—"

"It was a long shot, and you know it. Go back over everything. See if Victor found anything new. Talk to Mr. Morris. Maybe he's remembered something that he's willing to share. You never know what people will say when facing death or jail time. Whatever you need to do, do it. Now go home and start fresh tomorrow."

I stand and feel a little wobbly on my feet. I never was a good drinker. I pull the door open to the quiet precinct.

"Oh, and Jasmine?"

I turn a little too fast and hold on to the wall. Tyler looks at me seriously.

"One, get a rook to drive you home. Two, you ever pull that shit with a lawyer again and you'll be suspended without pay. Are we clear?"

"Crystal."

I walk out of his office and lean on the door, partly for balance, and the rest to gather my thoughts. I don't understand how a case with so much physical evidence is all circumstantial. It's annoying. Technology has never been my friend, but this is just plain obnoxious. It's like the blind date who doesn't take the hint when you give him the phone number of the local gas station or something. When they come across you by chance, they act like nothing happened. It's stupid. This case is a flashing neon sign of screaming Captain Obvious, and everyone is afraid to acknowledge the possibility of a connection.

Chapter Eight

The hallways always look the same. Dark, like out of a horror film. There's no fog or mist or anything like that, but the walls have a watery film on them. As if the building had a fire a few days ago, and it is slow to dry out. My mind is playing tricks on me again; this I know for a fact. Where I am, where I am going, I have no clue. Frankie always says to allow the dream to play out. They can be windows into the soul or a black hole sucking you into a darkness you can't escape.

A light at the end of the hallway; how symbolically played out by that brain of mine. I lift my feet over the garbage on the floor and jump when a rat scurries away. I'd run away too if I knew how. It's worse when they're this vivid. The light flickers in front of me. Walk in and face my inner demons or stay here, bang my head against a wall, and try to wake up.

Taking a deep breath, I lean back and swing my head forward, connecting with the wall. Ouch and fuck come to mind.

"I guess waking up is not an option at this point. Hey, Frankie, wanna wake me up?"

Silence.

"Yeah, great, the one time I'm not talking in my sleep."

Entering the bright light, my eyes fight to adjust to the change. Slowly, shapes come into focus; the slick walls show of worn, peeling paint. The floors are just as dirty, but no rats to be seen. Probably due to the light. It's then that I hear a whimper coming from my left. Turning around, I see a man lying on a rusted metal slab, his ankles and wrists bound. His skin is clean and his clothes missing.

Cop training takes over, and I jump three steps closer. Then my body stops—hard. There's a tray with various knives and other torture devices. One looks like a corkscrew for a wine bottle, others look like clamps, and some just look like something out of a medieval textbook.

"I brought you a present," the voice breathes onto my neck, the warmth causing my body to tense. My fists clench.

"None of this shit is real."

"It is if you believe it is."

"I don't."

He grabs my biceps and squeezes. My body tightens, waiting for an opening to attack.

"If you didn't, you wouldn't be here. Your body wouldn't respond to my touch, my breath on your neck."

His hands slide down to my wrists, and I am paralyzed. My brain says "attack, you can easily break a hold now," but my body remains still.

"How does it feel seeing him again?" His feet shuffle my body closer no matter how hard I try to remain at a distance.

"I feel nothing."

"Really?"

As we reach the slab, my body stops moving. Garrison walks around the assorted torture tools and looks at me.

"He didn't listen to you. You begged and cried your little eyes out, but he just took what he wanted."

"Dennis was my boyfriend."

"Yes, he was. Still raped you every chance he got."

Garrison looks at me closely, waiting for a response, but gets none

"Unless you liked it," he whispers as if it is taboo to say.

I can feel the anger in me boiling. One never asks to be abused, controlled, and taken against their will. Even if they do want to go down the kinky trail, there is always a way to get out of it with a password or code or some shit. I want to scream. I do. I want to wake up. I want these nightmares to be over.

Garrison picks up the corkscrew-looking tool and hovers over Dennis's body. He grazes the skin below the belly button and presses the sharp tip into the flesh. Red droplets form as a scream rips from Dennis's chest into the air. Every fiber of my being tells me to stop this, but I sit and watch. Every twist pushes the tool deeper. The screams get louder. They start to sound like mine.

"Jasmine, is that you? Baby, please make this stop. It hurts," Dennis says to the ceiling. His blindfold prevents him from seeing me.

"Please stop." The words come out of my mouth barely audible. I feel the tears hot on my cheeks. I don't want to relive this nightmare anymore.

"Why? He didn't stop when you asked. Repeatedly, I might add." He twists the tool slower, causing more torturous pain.

"I'm asking you to stop." My voice comes out a little firm this time, a slight confidence behind the words as my rational brain catches up to my anger. Garrison's hands stop. He walks behind me and slides his arms around my waist.

"You're right, I should stop. This isn't my battle to fight."

His fingers entwine with mine as he lifts my hand onto the corkscrew. My hand flexes with all my power, trying to distance myself from the device. The pressure of my palm pushes the tool deeper into the torn flesh.

"Fucking bitch, make this shit stop! I swear to God, when I'm free you're going to get it."

Times like these my mind floats away, far away where nothing can harm it. Even in nightmares, we need a safe place. It's where my family is, calm and at rest. Garrison's laughter brings my brain smashing back to reality.

My hand is covered in blood, the corkscrew so deeply embedded in Dennis's flesh it's hit bone. Garrison smiles at me, holds up a knife, and cuts one of Dennis's restraints. My heart races, my mind unclear. There's blood on my hands; how figurative. I've killed Officer James in self-defense, but his blood is still on my hands. I fall to the floor and crawl backwards until my back hits the wall. Something I've done many times in my life. Rocking back and forth, banging my head against the wall. Trying to wake myself up from this horrible dream.

My eyes open to see the side of my mattress. My knees are pulled to my chest tightly, and tears stain my pajama pants. My heart is unsettled and racing. My hands are clean, but they feel sullied. There's a darkness in me rolling around looking for a place. If I can't contain it, it will consume me.

***

The greenest lawns in the entire world are in a cemetery. Everything is perfectly manicured; the roads paved and pristine. For the morbidly inclined like myself, it makes it feel like the dead are better off. The grass is crisp, the flowers fresh, and it's quiet. You can think here. There is no judgment. Whatever happened before you entered these hallowed grounds are long forgotten. Then again, most of the stones in here have been forgotten. No one to kneel down and say farewell. No living family member who remember who they are, let alone where they are buried. Lives that meant so much to various people, whittled away to nothing more than a stone with a name on it.

No matter how hard I fight it, I know my stone will rest here someday. I know I will lie among my family, and Chase will visit for a time, but that will pass. Time will move on without me, and I will be nothing. There will be no footnote in history. No mention of Jasmine Steele anywhere. There will be bones in a box under a stone.

Tracing the outline of my mother's name, I promise as long as I breathe, I will not forget her. Even though in life, she forgot me. She gives me more comfort now being gone than I think she was capable of in life. She was so very tired. She needed to run away. I needed to let her. Now she is always here for me, even if she never replies.

"It's pretty here with the flowers starting to bloom, Mom. Lord knows Grandma would be sneezing her head off while trying to pick every damn weed that dared to break the dirt."

Leaning back on my heels, I look at my brother's stone, Henry and Belinda Steele, carved into a cold empty slab. The hurt and loss still linger, but less with each passing day.

"Chase looks more like Henry each day, but I swear his personality is all Belinda. His quick wit, humor, and his ability to beat me at video games. That is all your daughter-in-law. Don't get me started on his eating habits. Frankie swears he eats cookies like I did, but I never shoveled food into my mouth like that. He holds that fork like a fly swatter, ready to destroy whatever is on his plate. His appetite is outrageous too! Then again I never had a kid before so this could all be normal."

I mindlessly pull at the weeds hidden in the grass in front of my mother. I can feel the tears of frustration begin to form, and I truly want to fight them off. I know it's a war I won't win. I'm tired, drained. One hundred percent unequivocally shot. I don't know how much more my body can take. One way or another, I have to deal with my nightmares.

"You'd be going nuts right now, yelling at me for not sleeping and eating like crap. Probably telling me all about adoption, how hard it is here, and maybe a foreign child would be easier. If Henry was here, he'd be acting all protective, but things would be different. I try not to think about that now."

The wind picks up, causing a chill to race up my spine. Hadley would be telling me my family is here with me with every breeze. I'm more realistic. I know if they're somewhere else, they have better things to do than worry about me. The tears fall as the air hits my face.

"I wish you were here to help me. Sometimes I just wish I could hug you again, Mom. Just once . . ."

My cell phone annoys me, ringing at the most inopportune time.

"Steele."

"Ms. Steele, it's nice to finally speak to you."

"Who's this?"

"You've been digging around, Ms. Steele, and I don't like it. I feel since you have discovered so much about me, it's time to meet in person."

"Mr. Garrison, how did you get this number?"

"I have my ways, Ms. Steele. I will be at the park in an hour by the children's playground. You wouldn't shoot a man in front of children, would you, Ms. Steele?"

"It's detective."

"One hour, Ms. Steele."

Grabbing two rocks from the ground, I place one on either tombstone. My gut tells me I should call this in, but I'm stubborn like that. Some things you have to face on your own, like death. No one can save you from that.

***

Children have an innocence about them I wish I could have held on to. You know . . . just put it in a jar, letting a little bit out when needed. Relishing it over a longer period of time. Feels like it's wasted on the ones who know nothing. The rest of us adults no longer see the joy of rolling around the grass. There's no time; we're stressed, children demand attention. The ability to ignore everything around you and be truly happy is lost. The park still brings some joy to my heart, though. Like a distant memory, it's a flash and then it's gone.

Sitting here on a park bench, I envy those children in the park. They have no idea I'm sitting here. They have no concept of violent crime. They know slides, tag, and swing sets.

"This seat taken, Ms. Steele?"

I don't bother to look at his face. I know he looks like his son, the officer who tried to end my life. Just like the photos with a smug look of superiority.

"Garrison, you wanted me here. Talk."

"It's beautiful here, isn't it? My son Keith used to love it here. That's my park you know. When you killed my son, I donated the money to rebuild it in his honor."

"Your son shot me, Mr. Garrison. I cared so little about him, I never even knew his first name."

I can feel the older man tense next to me. This is a game of cat and mouse. The first to show weakness loses. I would prefer a stalemate right now. I don't trust what I would do if he cowered. I don't trust myself not to kill him.

"We've both made several mistakes in our lives. I'm here simply to offer my assistance with your investigation as a truce."

"What would you know about my investigation, Mr. Garrison?"

"Don't play coy with me. I know you have people digging into everything attached to me. What you'll find won't be useful, legally speaking."

"Money always gets people into trouble."

"If you can put the money on the person you are, in fact, accusing of said crime. You and I both know money is virtually untraceable. Regardless of your friends, this conversation will get you nowhere."

"Then what the hell are you offering me?"

"Harry Brandt or, as your techs know him, D.B.M."

Taking a calming breath, I force myself to focus on the children in front of me. I knew in my gut he was connected, but for him to openly admit when I can't use it in court pisses me off. He knew this when he came here. He's one-upped me, and I am forced to play his little game. I hate this shit.

"You funded his company."

"Yes, among other things."

"You know about his company's designs then."

"If you are referring to his open-source programs, yes. They have been used by several individuals I do business with. Mr. Brandt has handled a lot of this for me."

"He kill for you?"

I feel the bench shake as Garrison laughs at me. He's calmer since he's in control. It won't be pretty when I flip the switch.

"Mr. Brandt is many things for me, but a murderer is not one of them. He is hired help on a contractual basis. He's muscle, if you will."

"What about Walter Miller?"

"An old friend with a disgusting habit."

"You knew he was a pedophile and did nothing about it?"

"Ms. Steele, he wasn't going to have a plaything as long as he was taking my money, using my name for fundraisers, and more. I might not live up to your standards of a human being, but I do have limits. What he viewed in his private home on his own private devices was not my concern."

Seeing the kids laughing, I wonder if he sees how false that statement is. I tire of this conversation. He's worse than nonstick pans at this point. With all the circumstantial evidence swirling around him, nothing directly attaches his person to the crimes. So, even with all this information, a case against him won't hold up in court. I stand up and straighten my jacket. I need to put distance between the two of us. He has only fortified what I already knew. Either way, it doesn't make me feel any better.

"He works freelance for others who need things handled. When Walter decided the young woman was to be his, Harry had a change of heart. He asked for my advice."

"Kaley was raped and murdered," I spit out at him.

He turns his head and finally looks at me. His eyes look more human in person than I hoped. I wished he looked more evil, more vile. Yet, he looked just like anyone else in this park. I prefer my version of him.

"Yes, she was, before Mr. Brandt and I could handle things."

"You had Miller killed and sold his organs online."

He stands, looks at his watch, and smiles at me. There's the smug son of a bitch I was expecting to deal with.

"Mr. Brandt handled the situation. What he did to dispose of the evidence is of little concern to me. Now, you have your information about the person behind this hired job. I trust this will get you to calm your horses."

"You covered up my brother's murder. You can say whatever you want, Mr. Garrison, but this will never be over."

"I didn't say it was over, dear. I just said you ought to take a step back and focus on the case at hand. You won't be able to connect me to any of it. That I promise you."

He walks away from me, and I really want to pull out my gun and watch him fall to the ground. I feel that darkness rolling around in my gut again. I want to give in, fall into oblivion, but I have too much to fight for. Grabbing my cell phone, I dial Logan.

"Detective, how can I help you today?"

"I just had a meeting with our friendly financier. I need you to check into everything Brandt has at his disposal. Garrison threw him under the bus, and I want to know why."

"Maybe he's just expendable."

"Probably. Either way, he couldn't have run this entire operation on his own. He needs help. I want you to rip apart his company brick by fucking brick. And lock down all his assets. I don't want to know how, just make it happen."

"You got it, boss."

He hangs up on me before I can say anything more. Not like there's anything more to add. Mr. Garrison bothered me greatly. He pushes buttons in me I swore I would never allow. Maybe Tyler's right. Maybe I do want revenge instead of justice. Maybe I just need to invest in a Taser. That way I can make him squirm a bit. If my mother were here, she'd smack me in the back of the head. I can't tumble down the rabbit hole.

The house is dark by the time I come home. I ignore everyone for a bit. I need to just sit at the waterfront and clear my mind. There's so much noise in my mind from the frustration, it's hard to think straight. I try to be as quiet as possible, but the damn door squeaks when the seasons shift, and the house comes to life. Not in a good way either. Everything has a sound depending on the season. The floor sounds creaky one season and like a groaning old man the next. It is beyond annoying. Closing the door behind me, I feel the wall for an open key hook. I lock the door, but before I turn around, the light goes on, illuminating the room and blinding me.

"You could have told me you'd be late."

Turning around, I see Frankie sitting at the kitchen table, an empty whiskey bottle in the center of it. If she's been drinking, I am in deep trouble.

"Where were you?" She asks.

I open my mouth to speak, but she raises her hand, abruptly cutting me off.

"I don't want to hear about the case giving you stress. Don't lie to me, please. I think I've earned the right to ask for honesty."

She has and then some. Sitting across from her, I play with an empty shot glass on the table. Part of me wishes there was some liquor left. I'd take some just to feel it burn all the way down. To feel something other than this anger.

"I was at the cemetery today. Before you ask, no, I didn't want to bring Chase. I needed to go alone. I still do that sometimes. It helps me."

She stays quiet, her eyes never leaving mine. It's a bit overwhelming at times, her gaze. It's full of support and love. She lets me know in one look what many people search for in a lifetime.

"Irving Garrison gave me a call today."

She sits upright, her muscles tensing. I see her mood shift, but her eyes still show no fear.

"He wanted to meet me at the park."

"And of course you did." She tries to hide the sarcasm, but her voice betrays her.

"I know you're upset, but you know I had to. I needed to see his face."

"What did he want?"

"A truce. He wanted me to get off his back for a bit. In exchange, he gave me information about my case."

"He's not going to testify in court, so you basically put yourself in harm's way for nothing."

"He pointed me in the right direction. He also showed his cards in a way."

"That's not the point, Jasmine, and you know it."

"Brandt was behind the murder of Walter Miller. Miller killed Kaley."

"Can you prove it?"

"Brandt uses the software for a side business. Consider him the handyman of the dark web. It's a very lucrative side job."

"It explains a lot, but not enough. He already has millions."

"Not necessarily. His money is hidden. We're going to cut him off and see what happens. Maybe we'll get lucky and he'll make a mistake."

"How?" She stops herself.

She knows I've involved Logan before I can admit it. She leans back, obviously upset with me, trying to distance herself. I reach for her hand, but she slides it just out of reach.

"Does the rest of the department know about this?"

I don't answer, which in essence is one.

"If anything happens to him, Hadley will never forgive you. She's just getting her life back on track. She's been working on a new film, and Logan has been a huge part of that. If he gets hurt . . ." She doesn't finish.

"Kaley deserves justice."

"The man who killed her is dead. Justice was served in spades." Her anger is rising, and I don't know what direction this conversation is taking.

"And her little brother?"

That stops her dead. She knows I'm right. We need to finish this case so we can all move on.

"You need to focus on this case and let the rest go. You have to or you'll go crazy. I know you want to bring Garrison down, but you have to let someone else do it."

Before I can say anymore, Frankie leaves me alone with my thoughts. She'll calm down in time. She always does. I have to figure this all out before I lose my mind. I need to be able to focus on one case at a time. That much is true, but I need to be involved in bringing that man down. I don't know how, but I have to be a part of it.

Chapter Nine

I have always felt that sleep, like food, was overrated. It's a simple concept really. You eat only what you need to live, and you can sleep when you die. Frankie tells me I need to change my perspective about it all and just enjoy the little things. Seriously, I'm not a foodie. I hate cooking, and if it can come in shake form with all those vitamins I need, I'm good.

As I stare at the perfectly painted white ceiling, I can tell you honestly it is all a control issue. My job is one huge ball of stress and nerves. No matter how much I want to do a good job or help someone, I know eventually I'm going to fail. I have several cold cases in my drawers. Answering machine messages asking for me to open them back up. Tears and screaming children looking for their family member. Those are the worst calls. The kids don't know any better. The parents put them up to it but fuck if it doesn't eat you up inside.

Hell, just walking around the city, people spit on you, call you names, and taunt you. I'm not in uniform, but it's like they have X-ray vision and can see my badge in my ass pocket. I'm one of the good ones, but it doesn't matter. I'm evil because I carry a badge. I'm an equal opportunity victim. I'm gay and will rot in hell. I have a kid I'm raising in a sinful situation, again rotting in hell. I have a badge, so I'm a murderer, bad cop supporter, whatever. Once again, rotting in hell. On a case-by-case basis, I have a condo in hell.

The only thing I can control is my body and mind. I focus—sometimes obsess—over things too much, preventing myself from getting a good night's rest. I have to get these cases closed, help those people out. It's part of my DNA. If I fail, I won't eat or sleep until I do get it right. Frankie will cook, make me meals for work, and whatever else she can to help. I just get so involved in what I'm doing, I forget to eat or sleep.

Just like now. Except I know my body is not far away from cracking. I might end up in my condo sooner than I'd like, but I don't control that. Lord knows I wish I did. I wish He gave me that talent. Then again, according to many people, He doesn't listen to me anymore. So my head asks the question: Why has humanity forsaken me and my family when I have not left them? Maybe like me, they want some control in this world, and I refuse to relinquish it.

The light of my cell phone illuminates the room and breaks me from my daze. Grabbing the phone, I see Logan's name on the caller ID.

"Steele," I whisper, hoping not to wake Frankie.

"We locked down all of Mr. Brandt's financials. Based on what you told me, I decided to put a tracker on anything D.B.M. in the dark web. I was hoping for something to pop up, maybe an order or something. Anything connecting it to Harry Brandt."

"And?"

"Several encoded messages were posted on various boards ensuring that if an order had been placed, it will be filled. There's more, but I think it's best to not discuss it over an unsecured line."

"But you could tell me all of that with no problem?"

"It pertains to more sensitive materials. Hadley also told me physical graphs or charts make things a bit clearer for you."

Leave it to Hadley to explain my inability to program my DVR. She laughed at me once when I tried to fix the time on the damn thing. Then I realized the clocks moved forward, and it automatically changed. It was like Christmas when I realized I didn't have to fix it.

"I'll be there as soon as I can."

I expertly slip out of bed without waking Frankie. It's something us insomniacs are very good at due to loads of experience. Of course, getting dressed in the dark without kicking said furniture, that is something I have yet to master. Exhibit A would be my now stubbed toe and me hopping around trying to get the hell out of the room alive.

Leaning against the wall in the hallway, I see a flash of light come from Chase's room. He's got to be playing video games again. I'm all for playing at all hours, but he's been doing it a lot lately. I knock on his door, but he's got his stereo headset on. I sit on his bed, causing it to dip and him to jump a foot in the air. I point toward the television and shake my head. He turns to the screen in time to see his character get shot and die. He takes his headset off and gives me puppy dog eyes.

"Not going to work this time. I told you last time not to play this late."

"Well, actually you reminded me not to let Frankie know I play this late."

"Chase, don't make me have to be the bad guy and take the system out of your room. It's bad enough I get shit from all the other parents at your school telling me how it should be in the living room. Not to mention the 'Chase is too young to be online, you should have parental controls on it' bullshit. You're not giving me many options here."

"Aunt Jazz, half the kids from school allow parents to password protect the system. They all know the codes or how to hack them. We're not dumb."

"Yeah, well, I didn't need to know that"—I smile slightly—"but it does make me feel a bit better."

"Everyone sneaks games at night. Who do you think I'm playing right now?"

"Some random stranger who wants you to join some great new movement for independence in a third world country?"

"Funny, but no. My friends from school. We all sneak on at the same time."

"Okay, that's great, and I appreciate you not hanging out with some creepy guys from other countries, but enough. You have two choices: I tell your Aunt Frankie and she throws a fit. She might sell or destroy your system that cost me a hell of a lot of money. Or you can stop playing when it's bedtime. Choose wisely."

"Come on it's not like I'm—"

"Don't care."

"But maybe—"

"Not an option."

"Fine." He turns off the system. "I'm not happy about this."

"I'll talk to Frankie about allowing more game time on the weekends, okay?" He huffs and puts his headset away.

He lays back in bed, arms folded, pouting, his bottom lip stuck out ever so slightly beyond the top one. He definitely picked this up from Frankie. I don't pout; I just give in to Frankie because if she's happy, I will get what I want eventually anyway.

"Goodnight, pouty face."

I close the door and hear him huff one more time. I wait a few minutes until I hear his even breathing. He must have been tired to pass out that quickly. I wonder how many days these kids have been playing late into the evening. I guess now the question is do I let the other parents know or do I keep my mouth shut? Or do I tell Frankie, let her know I handled it, and let her deal with it? I'll take option number two. Anything to get me out of parental confrontations. Can't stand those.

***

A morning without coffee is a morning that should not exist. I'm sure I've said this plenty of times before, but damn I need a hot beverage to wake me up. Not to mention I am entering the domain of the intelligent technology people; I need to be awake. Sadly, no decent coffee shop is open at this hour. I'm desperate, not dumb. Here's praying that the tech guys appreciate good coffee or they explain things on a Sesame Street level. I doubt my brain could handle more of the technobabble.

"Detective, right on time!"

Logan whirls past me and uses his butt to open the doors. It's then that I notice he's holding two steaming mugs of coffee. As I pass him, he hands me one. I'm a coffee snob, so one must sniff said coffee and make sure it isn't a watery mess.

"I assure you, Hadley let me know your specific roast. It also happens to be my favorite, so it's nice to share a very smooth but seriously strong cup of coffee with a colleague."

It smells like heaven. I must look like a kid on Christmas morning because I feel my smile stretching from ear to ear.

"You brew good coffee down here?"

"The perks of having the newest tech gear. We demand proper coffee to ensure a happy work environment. Trust me, sitting here and staring at binary code is just not very entertaining. Don't get me started on following social media accounts, cell phone pings, and crap like that. It's fun to disprove alibis, but sometimes we just want to play games on these new computers. Could you imagine a game on that massive screen out there? We can even break it up into smaller ones so we all could play at the same time."

He looks at me, and I know he's been talking, but he lost me at bi-something-or-other code. I'm just figuring out how I can make a trip down here every day to get a proper cup of heaven.

"I lost you, didn't I?"

"Coffee, simple pleasure. You want to talk other stuff, hit Chase up. He understands it. I make him program this new smartphone thing. It's not very smart when I continuously lock myself out of it. He says he made it easier to open with a pin, but I promise you I'll forget that eventually."

"They're not really difficult. Maybe we can set you up with a better method . . ." He stops talking. It might have to do with me staring at him with a blank expression. While I appreciate the assistance, and it's nice he's trying to be kind to me, seriously do not try to teach me technology. Just quit while you're ahead.

"Gotcha, no tech classes. Maybe Chase and I can play some games though."

"I'm sure he'd love that. Now, beyond this amazing coffee, please tell me why I am here at this ungodly hour."

"Right." He places his coffee down and flips open his laptop computer. After he types away for a few seconds, the white wall behind him becomes his desktop screen. I have to admit that's a bit cooler than just showing me his small-ass screen. It makes it a lot easier for my contact laden eyes to see. He sits next to me and taps away on his screen. A few markers appear in a cluster on the screen. They could mean anything, but they seem to be centered around one specific area.

"What are those?"

"After you told me to attack everything to do with Mr. Brandt, I began tracing his phone and what towers it pings off of. I've also had the team searching through the encoded emails and figuring out who the buyers were, when meetings were made, times of deliveries, etcetera. The red markers are where a cell phone pinged off a tower at the location of delivery. It is always in the same spot and always a minute or two before the meeting time. The blue markers are where the traffic and other cams picked up the car that appears to be associated with the cell phone."

"They all seem to center around the park."

"Yes, it seems like that is the center of the operation. It's perfect."

"How is that perfect? It's in a public arena, people can scream, call the police, report suspicious activity. That is far from perfect."

"No one reports anything. Unless it's an Amber Alert, people will ignore anything and everything that doesn't directly relate to them. They're too busy looking at their own cell phones, texting someone, or updating their status somewhere. The point is, he's hiding in plain sight."

"That's not normal."

"Not for your average criminal, no. However, this is a technology-based criminal. They know statistics better than most."

"If they were so smart, why would they leave their cell phones on to be easily traced?"

"That's the concerning part. We've been able to identify some buyers. Their cell phone pings the nearest tower and stays there for the same time as prior transactions. The difference is that during these trans-actions, there is no other cell phone. If you watch the pings, they are consistent, they are parallel for over five minutes. Then they break apart."

"I don't see Mr. Brandt making that mistake. He seems to be sure of himself. Not to mention a person dealing with the underbelly of society with a multimillion-dollar tech company would not make a newbie mis-take like that."

"That was my thought, so we ran the phones. The main one is a burner phone, but we have actual contact information for the rest of them."

"What were the deliveries?"

"Drugs, guns, illegal information, women, organs, and sometimes ba-bies. It costs less to buy an organ or a child on the dark web than it does to do it legally."

"Like Mr. Morris."

"We tracked his phone as well. His meet was at the piers."

"Surgery in a cargo container?"

"You'd be surprised what's available in those things. That isn't the best part though."

"Hit me with it already."

"Irving Garrison owns the storage area."

"I'm going to go have a conversation with Mr. Morris. You keep digging in on Garrison. He wants me to back off. That means kick it into high gear. Watch your back. I don't want to explain to Hadley that you were hurt."

"If there is one thing my investigations have shown me, Mr. Garrison is not one to get his hands dirty."

"He's a starfish; he can cut off his limbs as needed, but they always grow back."

"Of all the things you could come up with, you chose a starfish?"

"I'm going to go have another conversation with Mr. Morris. You don't hate on my bad analogies. Chase loves them."

"Yes, well he's also a child living under your roof, so . . ."

"Funny. Call me if anything pops. And . . ."

"Keep tabs on the mastermind via the DL."

Confusion must have slowly etched its way across my face because Logan looks like he is fighting a fit of giggles.

"Don't worry about it, boss. Just go."

He waves me off and I leave. At a certain point, one must accept age is a problem. Younger people could easily pick up a device or the newest gadget and figure out how to use it. As we get older, busier, and stuck in our ways, new things fall into the "what the fuck" category. Like why the hell do I need a watch that extends my phone? I don't need a status symbol. I don't follow the masses. I don't want to talk to my wrist; that is what a damn earpiece is for. Most importantly, I wouldn't know how the hell to turn it on. I'm only in my thirties, but this crap makes me feel old as dirt.

***

I hate fate. I hate karma. Hell, I hate death, even though I obsess about it. Everything is out of my control, out of my hands, my mind, or my ability to change it. Why give me a mind to think and sort out a problem if you rip away the things I need to solve something? It's like dangling a lifesaving surgery in front of a patient's face. You know they need it, but insurance refuses to pay for it.

Watching the nurses rushing in and out of Morris's room, I feel the slap of death across my face. Like a force of mass destruction, he always gets his victim. You can push him away, hide from him, maybe even cheat him once or twice. I know for a fact that he will find you. You can only run so far on this plane. He can outlast you. That's why death is fascinating. He has a plan that only he understands. It has no rhyme or reason.

I'm known as a hard-ass detective you can't deny. I get to the bottom of a case, and I never give in. It doesn't matter if it's a cold case or not, I will get answers. As the alarms continue to blare in the hospital room, I feel just like him. I embody him. I have no rhyme or reason to how I do what I do. I just feel it, that need to solve something. I feel the need to protect the victims, their families.

"Detective? We did everything we could. He couldn't fight off the infection."

"What infection?"

"Mr. Morris had a cold."

"Death by sniffles? Forgive me, doc, but you are going to have to give me a bit more than that."

The two uniformed officers try to stifle a laugh at the doctor's expense. One stern look from me and they stop. Like I said, my reputation precedes me.

"The original surgical procedure was not as sterile as it should be. Couple that with organ rejection; we had him on a serious round of antibiotics and steroids. Simply put, his immune system was shot. That's why he was transferred to the ICU."

"You mind telling me everything you know?"

"I have other patients that need attending to. Everything you need to know is in my report. I'm sure the coroner you have will be able to explain it more in detail."

The doctor brushes past me as another alarm rings out above me. Death is working overtime today. Grabbing my phone, I dial the only person who obsesses over death more than me.

"Jasmine, darling, I swear I didn't finish all the Girl Scout cookies! If Chase told you that, he's lying."

"Okay, first, our defective organ recipient Jake Morris is dead. Second, you finished my Thin Mints? That is not cool. Finally, you are putting the blame on a child. That's sad."

"Right." Victor clears his throat. "I'll send my people to pick up the poor bloke. I'll also get more cookies as soon as I get the chance."

"I'll be following your men back to the lab. Maybe you can enlighten me how a simple cold can kill someone."

"Of course."

"And Victor, living with me does not mean eating my secret anti-health-food stash. Understand? You eat it, you replace it. Simple rule."

"Got it. I'll see you when you arrive."

Disconnecting the call, I look around the ward. A nurse with a mask on her face is slowly cleaning up the body, something they shouldn't be doing.

"Excuse me!"

The nurse stops on a dime but doesn't look at me.

"I need you to stop what you're doing. The coroner's office is coming to pick up the body."

She nods, looks up briefly, and exits the room. I swear I've seen her before; the eyes look familiar, but I can't place her. The officers walk into the room and just stand there.

"Anything you need from us, detective?"

"Yeah, one of you get me the security footage for this entire ward for today. Something doesn't feel right."

One of the officers ducks out of the room. He was turning a shade of green, so I'm sure it's more out of self-preservation than desire to complete the task. The other officer just stands there, calm and almost at attention.

"Tell me what happened."

"The nurse came in to check on him. She spoke to him a bit, touched him, and walked out. Guy was smiling at her. A little while later, the machines started screaming. Doctor came in and yelled some code out. They shocked him a bunch of times, and he died."

"Okay, get the crime scene unit over here. I want everything bagged, tagged, and dusted. If it isn't nailed to the floor, I want it at the lab."

"And if it is nailed to the floor?"

"Detach it."

The officer walks out of the room a bit irritated, but seriously, what kind of dumb question is that? I swear we need to raise the criteria for the academy. Either they're getting dumber, taking selfies with a dead body, or they're acting like hot shit with a badge. They make the rest of us look bad.

Two men from Victor's lab walk in to pack up the body for transport. After verifying who they are, I simply move out of the way and watch them wrap him up. The way they remove the body bag and place Morris into it is very graceful. Almost a peaceful transition. Unlike the nurses and doctors, who mutilate the body to try and keep it alive, these people are gentle. Hopefully when I die, they will be this careful with my corpse. Unless I die some gruesome way. Then Victor will just curse me to my condo in hell as he tries to reassemble me. Sadly, that thought makes me laugh a bit.

***

Considering the heavy nature of death, one would not necessarily expect to find a human being enjoying their job. They've never met Victor, the lovely coroner. Hearing the latest Taylor Swift song on the speakers is one thing. Watching Victor sing, dance, and shimmy his way around the body is another. If any authority figure was down here, they'd crucify him. I know better. He works best when he's relaxed, not thinking but doing. Our instincts make us better at our jobs. The suits upstairs always forget what it's like to be where we are.

"I know you're not into men so stop staring at my ass and get in here!"

Victor always had a way of knowing where I am. Except when he's drunk; then he doesn't even know where he is. Entering the morgue, I pick up the remote and kill the music. Nothing against Ms. Swift, but I need to hear the report.

"You turned off my music?"

"My ears are old, and it was too loud."

He lifts his face mask and shows me his full pouty lip. Did that ever work on his soon-to-be ex? I guess my lack of a response made my point. He shakes his head, causing the shield to fall in front of his face.

"You're no fun."

"Chase doesn't like me in multiplayer mode either. Sucks to be the both of you."

"I thought you were following the van."

"I wanted to make sure to pick up the records. Didn't trust them to be sent over with the body or by email."

I drop the file on a different metal slab and look over Morris. The one thing I haven't gotten used to is how some people look after death. Some look peaceful, like my mom. It's as if their inner beauty was released after the stress and darkness left the body. Morris, he looks like he went nine rounds with a heavyweight champion and lost. Granted, some of the damage is fresh from the attempt to save his life. His scale-like reddish skin, the swelling of his stomach and face—nothing pretty here. His family will probably have a closed casket.

"Has the lab been given the bed sheets and anything else they need to process?"

"Yep, they're doing it as we speak."

"Good, I'll have to go over their findings and compare them with my own."

"Guy was in liver failure. Doc said the surgery site wasn't sanitary, so he was on antibiotics. Morris managed to get some kind of infection and with his weakened immune system, died as a result."

"Well, yes, that would have killed the man eventually."

"What do you mean, eventually?"

"Just what I said. Eventually the man would have died from his infection. The scarring around the liver was immense. I swear I found rust particles from dirty tools embedded in the scar tissue. I don't know if they would have been able to perform a proper transplant with this hack job. But that doesn't appear to be what killed him."

"Excuse me?"

"His heart shows signs of cardiac arrest."

"Okay, so he suffered massive cardiac arrest due to the infection."

Victor grabs the report and flips through the pages faster than I do with the morning paper. Finally stopping, he folds the page back and points to a line of chicken scratches with numbers. I just look at him, begging for an explanation.

"His echo and EKG were fine four days ago. Yes, he had an infection. Yes, he would have died in a week, maybe less. He shouldn't have died today."

"So what killed him?"

"Based on the lack of evidence, I would lean toward air embolism."

"That's hard as hell to do."

"Possibly, but considering he had an IV, anyone could turn it off and use the port to inject a massive amount of air into the bloodstream. Considering his state of demise, I doubt he knew what was happening to him at the time."

"The nurse at the scene was the last to see him alive. How much air are we talking about?"

"Depends. Based on timing and severity, anywhere from ten cc to twenty cc."

"English?"

"One or two full ten milliliter syringes worth. Whoever did this wanted him to die within minutes of the dose."

There's a new player in this old game. I knew those eyes looked familiar, but I'm racking my brain with no results. I've got to see what the lab has. Maybe there's some video or trace evidence that can shed light on the subject. Otherwise, no DA will arrest Harry Brandt for crimes when the defense can argue reasonable doubt. I know our leads are solid, but in a world of reality television and instantaneous result episodes, I'm screwed.

Chapter Ten

I was having a good dream for once. I know it was a dream because the New York Mets won the World Series, and I wasn't dead yet. I like a dream like that. Mindless, calm, and just plain fun. Friends all laughing around the television as the crisp fall winds chill the air. My ragtag family enjoying one of the many things that connect us. Our devotion to lovable losers, but that's another story for another day.

Glass breaking forces me to bolt upright in bed. Frankie continues to sleep soundly next to me. Sliding out of bed, I grab my handgun on the nightstand. Normally, I lock it up, but I must have forgotten last night. I walk down the hallway, gun raised. Pushing Chase's door open, I see the boy is sound asleep. I hear more noises from the basement.

Taking one step at a time, I walk down the two flights of stairs in silence. Muffled cries for help reach my ears, and I'm instantly frozen. Hadley. The temperature of the room plummets. and my breathing quickens. Closing my eyes, I try to focus my energy. Whatever is going on, Hadley needs my help, and I have to move forward.

Opening my eyes, the walls of my basement have become the peeling ones of my nightmares. I knew it was too good to be true. This is like 2006 when Carlos Beltran didn't swing on a three and two pitch. I put one foot in front of the other, closer to the loud screams echoing through the hallway.

"Who doesn't swing on three and two? I mean, you're supposed to protect the plate. You get paid millions of dollars to protect the fucking plate."

"He thought it was a ball," Henry says to me calmly.

"Great, you're here too? Why can't my nightmares be about simple things? Like drowning or a plane crash? Why do I have to have friends in danger, freak outs, and a family member being my conscious? And I don't care what he says, if he swung and missed, I'd be prouder than watching the ball pass me by only to be called strike three. That was a weak play. Just like Glavine giving up seven runs in an inning and telling me it's just a game. He didn't pay over a hundred bucks to see his ass fall down at work. I would have been fired if I fucked up that much!"

"Tell me how you really feel."

Lowering my gun, I run my left hand through my hair. These dreams are taking their toll, and I don't know how much more I can handle. My right hand shakes holding my weapon. It feels foreign to me. I almost feel afraid of it, if that makes any sense.

"Eventually you have to face what you've done and accept it. Or you can fall down the rabbit hole and never come out."

"I've faced it and dealt with it."

"You feel responsible for Hadley. For her being hurt and for avoiding her. It's part of your DNA, Jazz. You wouldn't be you if you didn't care that much."

Raising my gun, I ignore my shaking hands and my brother as I trudge down the hallway. The door is slightly ajar, but I can see Hadley on the floor, beaten and bruised. I push the door open with my left foot, my eyes falling on Keith Garrison and Officer James in full uniform.

"Look who finally decided to join us," Garrison taunts me, his hands dripping with blood.

"You want to take a few shots? We'll hold her down for you," James says to me calmly. I never lower my weapon.

"You were supposed to protect her." I stare at James, anger rolling off me in waves.

"I did. I offered her a good life, a pampered one. She was all 'I'm independent' crap, so I did what I was paid to do. Trust me, if she came with me, this bitch would be barefoot and pregnant on a beach somewhere."

Hadley cowers on the floor, blood trickling out of her mouth. Her injuries seem so much worse than the night James and Garrison kidnapped us.

"She would have killed you while you slept," I reply calmly to him. Hadley is one hell of a strong woman; she would never allow him the pleasure of touching her.

"He would have had help, detective." Garrison leans against the wall, smiling. The anger in me wants to shoot him in the face. Then there'd be no smile on his face ever, but that isn't rational. Neither is fighting with your nightmares.

James lifts Hadley off the floor and pushes her up against the wall. She squirms beneath him, whimpering incoherent words.

"Let her go." I aim my pistol at James.

"Detective, how are you going to handle both of us?" Garrison continues to be smug. My rational is fading and my desire to kill him rising.

Hadley screams, and before my brain can catch up, I pull the trigger.

It clicks. I drop the clip and find it empty.

Anger boils over, and I spin the gun in my hand, handle first. I swing at James and hit him in the head. The cracking of bone echoes around the room. His lifeless body falls to the floor. Hadley slips down the wall, pulling her knees to her chest. Henry walks to her, kneels, and wraps an arm around her. My eyes look through my lashes at Garrison. Good must defeat evil.

He charges at me, but my instincts take over. I slip to the side and trip him. He falls face first, and I slam my knee into his back. There's nothing in this room to tie his hands with, and there's no way anyone is meant to leave this unscathed. Grabbing the sides of his head, I look at my brother. He just stares at me. With a quick movement, his neck snaps like a celery stick.

Falling to the floor, looking at my bloody hands, I realize I've killed them both. The bodies slowly deteriorate into piles of dust on the floor. The light flickers above, and I look at my brother.

"Don't go down the rabbit hole, Jazz. For your friends, Frankie, and most importantly Chase. Don't let them change you."

"I killed a man. How do you come back from that kind of darkness?"

"A true savior is one who has dark and light inside of them with the ability to keep them in balance. Be that person, Jazz."

My head is heavy, my breathing labored, my body weak. I hit the floor before I know what's happened. The coldness of the tile seeps into my skin, causing my teeth to chatter. Rolling my head to the side, I see Henry and Hadley are gone. I'm alone in this dark, dank room. Just like life: you're born alone and ultimately die alone. It's the middle where you have the most warmth, if you can hold onto it. My eyes close.

The cell phone on the nightstand screams at me to answer it. Opening my eyes to the familiar white-painted ceiling of my bedroom, I grab my phone.

"Steele."

"Detective, it's Logan. Thought you might want to come down here. We've scoured through hours of footage and Morris's computer. Found some minor things."

"I'll be down there soon."

I disconnect the call and look to my right to see Frankie still sound asleep. Looking back to the ceiling, I take a deep breath. I feel . . . rested, and that scares me. I killed two men in a nightmare, and I slept well. That can't be normal.

***

No matter how many times I walk into this room, I feel like I'm in another world. Sure, I've probably said that once or twice before, but the feeling never fades. I see Logan over by the mini kitchen area. Tech geeks seem to get everything I sadly want. He leans back and smiles at me, holding up a mug. I simply nod in response. The man is quickly gaining points for being an all-around nice person. Even though I want to be the protective good friend and grill him, I can't bring myself to do it. He's honestly one of the good ones, and he can help me level up my game.

"One dark roast with milk, no sugar." Logan hands me a mug and leads me to his office.

"Thanks, coffee is always appreciated."

"Hopefully what we found will also be helpful."

"Would be nice. I'm a bit tired of running all over hell and back trying to get ahead of this."

"Understandable."

He stops at a colleague's desk and hands the woman a small USB flash drive. She clicks it into her computer. I feel like the technology specialist's hands fly faster than a bug does when you try to kill it.

"The main thing to note is that Morris's computer really didn't have a lot of information on it. He spent a lot of time on the dark web, searching for anyone to save his life. He had emails from several doctors insisting he was on the list, but due to his past indiscretions, he was less likely to get the next available liver. He offered money to anyone who would give him a piece that was compatible."

"Well, the docs said the liver can regenerate itself, so you can have a living donor. Morris only had a part of it, right?"

"Yes, which would beg the question, where are the rest of his organs?"

"Can we find that out?"

"If we had access to the main seller's computer, possibly. After that though, what do you do with the information? Do you arrest the people for black market dealings? Put them in prison for trying to live?"

"I don't know, but we'll cross that bridge when we come to it. I was more concerned about those shitty surgeries and possible rejection patients that have no idea what's wrong with them. Maybe they couldn't afford real health care after buying this thing."

"You get me Harry Brandt's computer, I can probably find out the recipients."

I take a sip of the glorious coffee, and I let Logan's words sink in. He specifically asked for Harry Brandt's computer.

"How do you know he was the mastermind?"

"Lots of speculation, and Mr. Morris was not very good at making his transfers look inconspicuous. Most people will funnel the money through a different bank account or use cash, maybe even an anonymous wire transfer. You never use your personal accounts."

"Morris paid Brandt through his personal account, leaving a trace."

"A rather stupid move. He openly admits in an email that he sent the money to the company account by mistake. The response was a swift threat and orders on how to wipe the information from his personal computer."

"Obviously he didn't."

"No, he did, but you can't delete transactions or remove them totally. Brandt knew this; that's why there is an open-source code for money transfers in his program. If you happen to use your personal account, you run it through the program. It keeps everything anonymous and untraceable."

"So he was overly excited, didn't think, and paid in advance."

"And paid the price. Morris purchased an organ that was his blood type and was written as being from a young woman. The listing, the description of the victim, none of it matches Walter Miller."

"Brandt switched the liver donations as punishment."

"It wouldn't be the first time. That would also explain why Mrs. Morris informed me her husband's office had been broken into and ransacked. They wanted this laptop."

"She never mentioned it to us."

"A lot of people talk to us because we look less copish. They know we work for the same team."

"Either way, Brandt had to know we would track the financials."

"Yes, but they look like normal transfers without the purchase information and emails. Any defense attorney would rip me a new one on the stand."

Logan looks down at the woman sitting patiently at her computer. He nods at her, and she clicks a few things on her computer. The main screen on the wall shows the hospital footage.

"We got lucky with the footage. Can you zoom in on the IV port?"

The clip zooms in, and it is a bit grainy, but you can make out the details. The clip plays as the nurse pulls a syringe out of her pocket, pulls the plunger, and then injects it directly into the port. She repeats the action a second time.

"Victor was right. Morris was murdered."

"It gets better. Zoom out and fast forward to after Morris's death."

I watch myself and the officers mill about the room. The nurse leaves the room. She pulls out a cell phone and types on it before putting it back in her pocket.

"Who did she message?"

"We traced it to a burner cell, but that isn't the good part."

I drink the coffee, expecting him to continue, but he doesn't.

"What's the good part?"

"We have facial recognition software, and we decided to run the nurse's face through the database."

"How would that help? Her face is partially obscured."

"Yes, but the features of her face are the same. Her sunken eyes, high forehead, pronounced jawline and high cheekbones. Bones and science never lie. We got a match."

The monitor pops to life, and I stare at the image of Kiernan Jones on the massive screen, her eyes popping out of the screen, and I remember those eyes. She was the obnoxious twit behind the counter, a perfect cover from the police.

"It gets better. The cell phone pings I told you about before? They were hers. I don't know how she is involved, but she is a part of this."

"If you find anything else, let me know."

***

Sitting behind my desk, I stare at the whiteboard with all the information under the photos. It's an archaic way of doing things, but it works for me. Rubbing the back of my neck, I'm trying to come up with a plan of attack. How can we go into Brandt's office without spooking either of them?

"Can I come in?" Will says from the door. I lean back and wave him in. My words are failing me as my frustration grows.

"So, I hear we have a raid planned for tomorrow."

"Yep. Just have no idea how the hell we're going to handle it."

"Captain is over with the DA trying to expedite a warrant. I don't think Brandt's lawyer is going to make this one disappear."

"No, but we have to be smart about how we go in. You and I know the floor. If there's a hail of bullets, too many innocent people will get hurt."

"The leader of the team has blueprints of the building. He's made an optimal route to the floor, plus how to evacuate the other floors in case excessive force is necessary."

"One thing has been irritating me. What the hell does D.B.M. stand for?"

"Does it matter? All killers like to have nicknames. Makes them more official."

"Not really, but it means something to me."

Leaning back in my chair, I put my feet up on the corner of my desk. My eyes stay focused on the whiteboard. All those connections—every bit of information—all points to one man running the show. I think Will has slowly started to believe me that Irving Garrison is that puppeteer, but we can't connect him. We don't have enough evidence.

"He'll trip up. You just have to be patient. One case at a time." My eyes focus on Will. He's staring at the board as well, having moved his chair.

I've gone off the handle a bit this entire case. Luckily, it didn't cost me the people who support me the most. Like my brother said, I can't go down that rabbit hole, no matter how appealing it is to walk up to a vile human being and remove them from the world. There would be less pain. Less hate. Less evil. Less of everything negative that seems to rule the world.

But there is a problem with my theory. Eventually, I would become no better than the person I killed. I would remove people, for reasons only known to me. That vile human being is still someone's parent or son. That someone is still a living, breathing person. I would have snuffed out their ability to obtain a balance with light. One day, when I least expected it, someone would remove me from the world for being that very vile person that started the cycle.

It's a never-ending Ferris wheel with no ability to get off. Life sucks that way. You can't choose how fast you spin. You can't control who gets into your car all the time either. You just get on and pray you don't fall off the damn ride.

"When do they want to do this?"

"Early morning hours. It'll take that long to get a judge to sign off."

"Figures. In the meantime, they can destroy any and all evidence sitting in their offices."

"Jasmine, they've been doing that since we first came by. They're cocky, not stupid. I say we both go home and enjoy time with the family. Tomorrow's going to be a heavy day," Will says as he stands up and stretches.

I follow suit and stay silent as we walk out. My mind is full to the brim with theories and other random crap. I need another good night's rest. Maybe I won't have a nightmare again.

$$***$$

The house is quiet, but Frankie's car is in the driveway. The dinner table is set, complete with wine glasses. As I place my keys on the hook, the noise in the basement makes the bile rise up into my mouth, forcing me to swallow it back down. Dropping my bag, I rush down the stairs two at a time.

The door to my locked room is open. I must have forgotten to lock it the last time I was down here. I walk into the room, and my worst fear is revealed. Frankie stands there, one hand on her hip, the other covering her mouth.

"I can explain," I say, full well knowing I really can't explain an obsession to a psychologist. I won't sound normal at all.

"How can you explain all this?"

I walk into the room and place my hand on her shoulder. She shrugs me off and spins around. Her reddened eyes in her tearstained face lock onto mine.

"How long?"

"Frankie . . . "

"Just answer me! How long have you been sneaking down here and creating this . . . obsessive behavior?"

"A month or two after we moved here."

Her eyes widen, and she takes a step back from me. I can see her eyes darting all over the room. The doctor in her is working overtime, and I'm sure a lecture is to follow.

"You need to get rid of this. All of it."

"Frankie, you know I can't do that."

"I'm converting this room for storage of Chase's sports equipment. You don't have a choice."

Her voice is a tone I've rarely heard before. I know there's no room to argue, but I know myself. I'm going to do it anyway.

"I've put in too much time to just toss away all this work!"

"Work? This is obsessive behavior! People pay me a fortune to help them get over things like this. Not my girlfriend though; she just does it right under my nose. Here I thought you wanted a writing room. A place where you could go and be free of distractions. You lied to me—again."

That stops me. I lied to her again. I've been doing that a lot lately. How can we plan a future when I keep hiding things from her? I take a step back from her and lean against the wall.

"I have to finish this. I have to make him pay for what happened."

My voice betrays me. It cracks, and my fear is evident. I want to make it stop, but once the flood gates open, it's over. Frankie looks me over, runs her hand through her hair, and wipes her face. She walks up to me and places her hands on my biceps.

"How about we pack it away? You've done a lot of hard work and research. We can put it in a box for a later time. If something comes up, we'll have the information for someone else."

"But . . ." I try to protest.

"No, Jasmine, this is not healthy. I need the space for Chase's various sports endeavors, and you need to let this go. I'm not saying forever. I'm saying this way of doing things is done. I can help you. Victor lives here now, and then there's Will. You do not have to fight this alone. Let us help you."

I nod. She kisses my forehead and leaves the room. I know she's gone to get those plastic tubs we used to store old decorations in. My hideaway, my safe haven where I can air out my demons, is being taken from me. My heart is racing, and I really wish I could control it. This is what it feels like to rip off the Band-Aid. Maybe I am still that young girl whose mother took away her pacifier. I cried for hours every night until I learned to suck my thumb. Still have a scar on my thumb from that. Found solace in it until I was about ten. Mom never broke me of that addiction. Frankie is forcing me to go cold turkey.

This is going to be hell.

Chapter Eleven

I magine about fifty young kids at a small park vying for the slide. It's chaos. That's what the ground floor of Bridge the Gap's building looks like. There are trucks outside with the powers that be barking orders. Will and I are in front of the main barrage of personnel. Our case, we walk in first. Normally, they wouldn't let me do shit, but you don't mess with a Marine.

The vest is a bit tight on me, and I hate it. Will made sure it was as snug as could be. Something about protecting my body as much as possible. I get it, I do, but a girl has to breathe. He'll deny it, but since we've been working together, he treats me like his baby sister. I know we're equals; that isn't it. You just try telling a Marine that you're not a family when you head into enemy territory. You won't win that argument. He's my partner in crime, and the big brother I need. I just seriously wish he would understand a woman's right to have her boobs only squished for a mammogram.

"Okay, the teams are sweeping floor by floor," the captain says calmly.

"Heat signatures," Will pipes up.

"That's where we run into a slight issue. He's got someone with him."

"Any idea who they are? Kiernan? Another employee?" Depending on who that is, it might alter our plan of attack.

"I wish I could tell you. Whoever it is hasn't left his office. We've got a team checking the cars in the parking garage. If we find a visitor's pass, we'll run the plate. Might give us the information before you get to the top floor."

"If someone's in there, we need to get eyes on them."

The captain looks at me, and I can see the cogs moving in his brain. I know he wants to let me do my job, but his concern for my safety is holding him back a bit. Like I've said a million times before, we're family.

"What do you suggest?"

"Will and I go inside. We take the elevator and go inside like we've done many times before."

"Captain, Steele and I can relay information back to you. It might help move things along."

"Fine, whatever you do, the two of you do not engage the suspect. Do you understand?"

"Yes, sir," Will and I both utter quickly. We know we'll probably break that request, but what can you do? Life throws curve balls, but sometimes you have to swing.

"Pay attention to the voices in your ear. You hear anything you don't like, you get the hell out of there. Remember, you are only our eyes on the floor. We do this by the book."

The captain walks away from us. Will turns to me and starts tightening the Velcro straps on my bulletproof vest Nervously, I start doing the same thing to him. I don't want to explain to his wife why his vest slid and a bullet hit him. Not a conversation I want to partake in, ever.

"You coming?"

Without thinking, I start the walk to the building. My mind goes through random check lists. Leg holsters tight. My hands check the belts as I walk. Check. Guns are loaded, check. Earpiece in ear, chatter understood, check. Push all thoughts of Frankie and Chase out of your mind. It's then that I hear them laughing together. I've heard it so many times before, but right now that laughter makes me want to turn around and go home. I take a deep breath, push the sounds out of my head. Mind clear, check.

The elevator doors open, and we both enter, backs to the wall, facing the door. Will hits the floor number. He cracks his knuckles and then his neck. I can tell he's running through his random checklist now. It's calming knowing I'm not alone in this.

"Steele, Everts, mic check." The captain's voice echoes in our ears.

"Everts here," Will states. His tone is militaristic, emotionless.

"Steele here." I'm surprised that my voice sounds the same. Although the throat mic feels funny. I know Will said it was the best for this situation, but it feels like I'm choking.

He's rubbing off on me in a good way. The elevator doors open. Will steps out first, gun raised. I follow behind him. We quickly clear the lobby with tactical precision. He turns to face me and motions with his eyes. Anyone else would be lost, but not me. I am in awe at how easily our friendship has transcended words. We understand each other's moves.

Will and I each grab a handle on each side of the double doors. I nod, and we quickly slide inside them. The two of us fall to the ground and hold our hands out. We catch the doors and help them close quietly. Will waves his hands, points to the main office, and holds his hand level. I nod in understanding.

Keeping as low as possible, we walk around the wall and into the main area. Just as we enter the area, shots ring out, shattering the glass of Harry Brandt's office. The two of us drop down with our backs to the desks.

"What's going on up there?" I hear the captain asking, but it barely registers.

I look over at Will before leaning around the corner of the desk to get a better look. The long path between the rows allows me a clear view of Brandt's office. The lawyer sits tied to a chair, crying, her distinct moans muffled by the duct tape over her mouth. Leaning back, I realize we're in trouble.

"He's got the lawyer," I whisper over to Will.

"Call it in," he replies quietly.

"This is Steele, we have a situation up here."

"Go ahead, Steele."

"Brandt's lawyer is being held hostage. Full restraints. Shots were fired from his gun, shattering the office's glass walls."

"Do not engage," the captain says calmly.

"Sir, we feel—"

"Everts, I sent you and Steele up there to be our eyes, nothing more."

"Sir, he's acting like a rat backed into a corner. I'm concerned about the welfare of the hostage," I say mechanically.

"We are in position to negotiate, sir," Will offers.

"Everts, I understand you want to help this woman, I do, but we don't know what we're facing. If what you two said is true, this guy is really good at covering his tracks. Let us clear the floors before you open your mouths. Udall out."

Will closes his eyes and takes a deep breath. This is not what the two of us signed up for. Well, it sort of is, but on paper only. You never really want to be a part of it. This is no longer a simple wait and see to us. The idea of an easy arrest is out the window. I hit my head against the desk, causing something to fall to the floor. The shattering noise fills the room. I look over to Will and mouth "I'm sorry." Even now I can easily make a mistake.

"Who's out there? You the fucking cops? I won't come easily. You want to take me in, you have to go through this bitch first!"

I look over at Will, and he knows exactly what I'm thinking. I'm rather thankful for it, considering this large pile of shit we find ourselves knee-deep in. He shakes his head at me, and I turn away from him. I know what the rational side of my brain is telling me.

"Captain, cover is compromised. We need a negotiator to call or get up here ASAP."

"Negative, we are evacuating the building. All personnel are to retreat to the lower floors."

"Sir." I raise my voice slightly. "We need someone to help diffuse the situation."

"Jasmine." His voice is soft. "I need you and Everts to take the stairs and get out of the building now."

"Captain…"

"This is not an option. This is an order."

"Explanation?"

"The building is wired. Bomb squad found no trigger box. We had images sent to Pevy and the team. It's a secure wireless setup. They are trying to access the feed, but it will take time."

"Brandt has to have the trigger."

"It's a risk we're not willing to take."

"Then what's the play?"

"Nearby buildings are being evacuated. Once clear, we'll call Brandt. Meanwhile, tech is trying to isolate the signal and disrupt it."

"Steele out."

"Jasmine, you and Will—" I pull out my earpiece and ignore the rest. Will looks at me and does the same. I know the boss is in control, and he feels the best course of action is to wait. Will and I know it isn't because we're up here. Brandt is deranged and running off the deep end. We both understand one thing clearly: the lawyer's time is limited.

Will tilts his head and looks at me. One of us has to do this. It just depends on who stands first. It's like a stare down at high noon. Who is going to draw their pistol and fire? I take a deep breath and stand up. I look to my left, and Will is standing as well. He pushes me to the ground and makes sure to stare at me for a second. He's in the open, so I have to have his back. I motion to the outside route around the desks. He nods and walks toward the office. I pray he knows what he's doing, or we both might end up on a table. Then our significant others would bring us back to life just to kill us again.

"You're that cop who's been up my ass." Brandt aims his gun at Will.

"Harry, I'm just here to talk." He holds his weapon above his head so Harry can see it.

"Take out the clip and toss it to the side."

Will slowly does as he's told. I hear the clip land by my feet. It's standard issue. I pick it up in case I'll need it.

"Empty the round in the chamber."

Once again, Will is obedient. The bullet hits the carpeted floor.

"Now toss your gun away."

Will tosses the gun to his right, in the path I plan to take. Smart Marine. Doing the one move Will taught me that I hate, the snake crawl, I slowly navigate the desks unseen. I look at the floor and see Will has moved closer to the room. He's gotten way too far ahead of me. Not good.

"Stop. You stay there now."

"Okay, tell me what you want."

"This bitch was supposed to make it all go away. Was going to hire someone to fix things, but no, she's letting me go down alone."

"We know you didn't act alone, Harry. Kiernan, she was helping you?"

I reach out and grab Will's gun, reload it, and place it in my empty holster. I hear the pause in Harry's voice. He didn't know his receptionist was in on it.

"What does she have to do with this?"

I go back to the snake crawl and maneuver my way around the floor. Coming to another desk, I sit up and take a peek. I'm about level with Will, but I still don't have a clear shot if I need to take one.

"She was seen at the park many times, at your drop-off point."

"No one knew about that."

"Her cell phone pinged the tower there several times."

"That bitch." He pulls on his lawyer's hair, and she whimpers. "Did you know about this?" She frantically shakes her head in the negative.

Crawling on the floor again, I manage to get myself into position quickly. A pretty damn good job, if I do say so myself. I look around and see some officers with riot gear waiting where Will and I started out. I try to get their attention carefully, but no one is paying attention to me. If they rush in, everyone is as good as dead.

"I had nothing to do with that shit. Whatever she did, I have nothing to do with it."

"She killed Jake Morris at the hospital."

"That alcoholic was dying anyway; what does it matter when he died?" Brandt laughs.

"She injected air into his IV tube. He didn't stand a chance. That's homicide. It's on her, not you."

"I had nothing to do with it, but I don't feel bad the bastard is dead. He wasn't worthy of life anymore."

I've got a clear shot, but my hand is shaking. I could shoot him in the leg. I could end this right now, but I can't. This is why I should have been the negotiator. Will could be sitting here right now, wondering whether to hit the tibia or fibula. He would never hit the femur since he had a buddy with that fracture. You're never the same again. Me, I'm just trying to aim and hit the man. Right now, it's worse than trying to hit the damn ducks at a carnival.

"Whatever happened, we can sit and talk about it. Just let her go."

"You think I'm an idiot? I want an untraceable car out front. She comes with me. When I get to where I want, I'll let her go. Free and easy."

Brandt holds his gun on Will. I watch him cut the restraints on the hostage. He pushes the knife against her neck and forces her to stand up. He pulls her back to his front. If Will wanted to overpower Brandt, it just became more difficult.

"Let me talk to my captain, and I'll see about the car, but I can't let you take her with you. My boss won't allow it."

Will slowly puts the earpiece in as Brandt watches him closely.

"Captain, Mr. Brandt here has a request for an unmarked vehicle . . ."

"Untraceable too," Brandt screams.

"As well as untraceable."

"We need the hostage in return, and we need time."

"Harry, my boss says the car might take a bit of time, but when it gets here, we need the hostage as an act of good faith."

"I'm not stupid, detective. Tell your boss if he tries to screw me over, I'll kill everyone here and whoever is outside."

Will's face doesn't change. I'm sure Brandt noticed this. because he's slowly moving to a back door. The hostage is blocking my shot.

"You know about my backup plan."

"Yes."

Without saying another word, Brandt fires directly into Will's vest. It knocks him down hard. Brandt hits the hostage over the head with his gun and rushes out the back door. I jump out from cover and rush to Will.

"I'm fine! Get him!"

I rush out the back door and fly down the steps as fast as I can. Looking down the railing, I see Brandt a floor below me. I continue rushing down lower and lower. No matter how fast I seem to go, Brandt stays one floor ahead of me. Finally, I hear a door open and slam shut. It's the last floor down, but not the basement. This was not on the blueprints.

Pulling open the door, I enter the dank room gun first. The walls remind me of my nightmares. Paint peels from the walls. The musty smell sours my stomach. I can feel the fear from my dreams creeping up on me. There's a flickering light at the end of the hallway half blocked by a door. There's no telling where Brandt is down here. I can't see too far in front of my face to tell if there are any offshoots from this main hallway.

I keep my stance firm, small steps, gun aimed straight toward the light. I hear Hadley's screams in my head. I know they aren't real, but they feel like they are. The light ahead flickers and goes out. I've got a flashlight in my cargo pocket, but I'm unsure if I should use it. If I click it on, Brandt will know I am here. If I don't, Brandt can get the jump on me. I wish I had night vision goggles.

I place my left hand on the wall, my gun still facing forward in my right hand. Slide left foot forward, slide right foot to meet it. I continue to do this while taking deep, calm breaths. I don't want to think about what my hand is touching on the wall. Mold, urine, feces, lead paint, or maybe even dried blood—all the options dash though my mind. Any normal human being would let go of the wall, but I'm not normal.

My left foot kicks the wall in front of me. Using my left hand, I feel around for the door and push it open. There's a small glimmer of light from the back of the room on the ceiling. Walking over to it, I kick a set of steps. I slowly climb up two steps. I grab my flashlight out of my pocket and switch hands holding my gun so I can take a swing at the light. The wood pops up and crashes back down. Using all the force I can muster, I ram my shoulder into the cracks and I hear a click. I push it open all the way. Sunlight floods the room from an alley. Brandt never left this way, but the light will help.

An arm quickly wraps around my throat and pulls me back down off the steps. I swing my gun backwards and hit nothing. I drop the flashlight as I try to pull the arm away. It's an interesting high when your brain starts to feel the loss of oxygen. He could snap my neck right now. My arm feels like I'm swinging through water, but my gun connects with his head. I fall to the floor hard, my brain desperate for air and not focusing on Brandt crawling up the stairs.

I drag myself to my feet and stumble after him. I hit the ground again, my body fighting me. Brandt struggles ahead of me, holding his head. I raise my gun and take aim. My focus sucks; it looks like there's two of them. I need to relax and breathe.

"Just aim slightly above your target," I whisper to myself. "Look for the back of the rim and let the ball go."

I fire. Time slows. My gun recoils, but I handle it. A scream pierces the air and Brandt falls to the ground. My brain finally catches up and allows me to slowly stand. I drag myself to his fallen form. His left leg is bleeding from the wound. I hear him laughing as I approach. That's when I hear it—the sound of bombs exploding a slight distance behind me. I look at his hands, but they are firmly holding the wound.

I kick his leg and force him to roll over. I slam my cuffs on him and drag him to his feet. He's going to hobble to a cop car. I'm not going to think about Will right now. Not until I know for sure if he was still in there. I can't.

"How'd you set it off?"

"I didn't." He winces in pain. "It was on a timer."

"You knew we'd try to disrupt it."

"You cops are always predictable. You might think you're one step ahead, but you never are. Just like I know I'll never stand trial," he says confidently.

I wordlessly accept his comments. If I was younger with less experience, I'd probably argue with him. Sadly, he knows too many people. He's too valuable. He'll either end up in federal custody or dead. Even if he does stand trial, the government might make a deal. In other words, they would stage it to look like a conviction followed by a prisoner killed by another inmate. It isn't uncommon, and people would think the score was settled. In the meantime, he'd be on some beach drinking Corona while I was hunting down another psycho.

The captain sees me and runs toward me with two officers in tow, yelling out commands. The officers grab Brandt and drag him away to a cruiser. The captain looks me up and down. He's probably trying to see if I have any new war wounds for the hospital to deal with. I wait, silently praying he will tell me the status of our team and the surrounding civilians.

"Everyone got out before it blew. Only minor injuries."

"Will?"

"Is at the hospital. The bullet hit him with some force. He might have a broken rib or two."

"He'll have a hell of a bruise but deny the rest."

"I shot another man, Captain."

"I know, but he's still alive. Meet me back at the precinct, okay?"

I nod my head and walk off. I just want to go to the locker room and take a hot shower. I need to disinfect myself, especially my hand. I need to wash the fear off my skin.

***

The captain opens his office door. I haven't spoken to anyone since the shooting. I know he's alive. I know he's going to have a hell of a recovery, but I didn't kill him. I wonder if that is what's eating at me. I know I was capable of killing him. I could have aimed the gun a bit higher, but I didn't. That makes me different from Harry Brandt and the entire Garrison family.

"You know the drill" the captain says somberly.

I grab my gun and place it in the plastic evidence bag. He seals it and looks at it casually. I'm waiting for the lecture. I want the lecture. Tell me anything, I don't care. I just need to know I did the right thing. I need someone besides myself to remind me.

"It was a good shot. You should have your weapon back by the end of the week. Do you have your secondary on you?"

"No." My throat is so dry. "It's locked in the case at home."

"No problem. When you come into work tomorrow, just use that gun. I'll make sure it's noted in your file."

"Thanks."

"You want to talk about it?"

I sit down in the chair and lean my elbows on my knees. The captain sits next to me, waiting for me to say something, but I have nothing to say. Maybe it's because the words don't come or because I'm emotionally shot, but I start to cry. The tears roll silently down my face.

I feel the captain place a hand on my shoulder. The damn breaks and, burying my face in my hands, I crumble. It's as if all the stress, fear, and pressure oozes out of my body. I don't gag or cough. I just shake violently as the tears fall down my face. The captain pulls me into a hug, and I feel myself start to calm.

"It's okay, Jasmine. I promise you it'll get better."

"You don't understand, Tyler."

I pull away from the captain and lean back in the chair, staring at the ceiling. "I wanted to kill him," I whisper.

Tyler's eyes widen for a second before he relaxes back in his chair.

"My fourth case on the force, we got a call about a floater. So, my partner and I go down to the pier, and we see this white blob floating in the water. He says it's trash, but I walk to the steps and use a pole to try and pull whatever it was closer to me. I managed to grab onto some cloth and got it close enough. It was stuck on the side of the pier. When I poked it again, it rolled. The body was so swollen, the skin peeling, I thought it was butcher's meat since we were in the district. It wasn't until the washed-out gray eyes stared at me that I freaked out. I was screaming at my partner. He comes running down, screaming to dispatch everything I told him. When they finally come down to the scene, they pull the body from the water. Coroner said it was a young male, at most nine years old. Most of the evidence had washed away, but they had dental records."

The captain stands up and walks behind his desk. He sits down and pulls open a drawer. I watch him search for something before he drops a file on his desk.

"Edgar Flores was reported missing the day we found him. Doc said he had to be in the water for longer than that. I'll never forget the greenish tint to his skin. He looked like a zombie in some horror movie with Hadley. Anyway, since we found the body, my captain wanted us helping the detectives on the case. So, there I am, working alongside the best of the best, and my partner is a know-it-all. Williams, the lead detective, sends the two of us to interview the family. They'd already been notified, and there was no way they were going to ask for them to ID the body."

The captain opens up the file and pulls out a photo. He holds it up respectfully. He leans forward and hands me the photo, then leans back in his chair again.

"When I went to see his parents, they gave me that photo. Asked that we keep it with the file. They wanted us to see the young boy, not the mutilation. I understood, but my partner was such a fool. He acted like hot shit, almost accusing the parents of murder. I finally told him to look at the boy's room while I continued the investigation. After two months, we had evidence leading to a young college student named Justin Bartlett. He was well known around campus as having a young boy fetish. Justin was a scholarship student, no connections to the community. Nothing stopping him from running. We argued with the DA, but without any hard evidence, they wouldn't hold him. We didn't have DNA or all this technology. It was easier to commit a murder and walk away. Trial date comes, and I'm waiting in the hall. DA comes out and pulls me aside. Asks me if I know where Justin is. I had no idea. We searched high and low, but the man had no ties and fled. I had to tell his parents."

He turns the file around and pushes it toward me. I take it carefully and scan over some of the yellowed pages.

"Every time a young boy was found, I made sure to watch the case. I wanted to know if Justin surfaced. I wanted to bring him in. In the back of my mind though, I wanted to bring him into a dark alley and beat the shit out of him. Then, I wanted to put my gun in his mouth and scare him. Then I'd kill him."

"I feel that way sometimes too."

"But we don't. That's the important part, Jasmine. We are better than the average murderer on the street because we care enough to let the bastards live. Forgive yourself."

"Did you ever find him?"

"I came across his picture a few years ago. He died in a drunk driving accident."

"Figures."

"He was sober."

Karma strikes again. I place the photo back in the folder, close it, and put it on the desk.

"What happened to your partner?"

"Killed in the line of duty. He was a pompous ass, but he became one hell of a cop." I stand up, nod, and head to the door.

"Tech seized Harry Brandt's laptop. They're going over it all. There might be something in there that's useful to you."

"Thank you."

"Jasmine, just remember there might be a case you can't let go of, but you can't let it rule you."

I don't reply. I want to talk to Logan now. I don't want anyone else touching the laptop. He knows what I need. He's my dealer, and if I want to let this go, his answers are my fix.

Logan is waiting for me in his office, which shouldn't surprise me. I walk in expecting to hear some protests or calming words, but he just looks at me.

"Detective, I assume you're here for the laptop."

"Only you."

"It's just me in here, yes."

"No, only you touch the laptop. I don't want any information lost. If you can connect Brandt to the murders with his own laptop, that's life without parole. If you happen to find more, that's excellent for me."

"Yes, well that might be difficult."

"Why's that?"

"It's encoded in a way I have never tackled before. I truly don't know if I or any member of our team can break it."

"Do your best, that's all I ask, and make a copy. Just in case there's some back-door bullshit that deletes everything."

Logan smiles at me as he stands and walks around his desk.

"Aww, you thought of modern technology in an understandable way. I'm so proud of you."

He goes to hug me, but I take two steps back.

"You might be dating a very good friend of mine, but no hugging."

Logan holds his hands up and walks back around to his chair. He rubs the back of his neck and cracks his knuckles before going back to work.

"I'll let you know if I find anything."

"Thanks."

"Now, if you'll excuse me, I have to call my girlfriend and explain that my slave driver of a boss demands I work late."

"Funny."

"She won't get mad if I blame you. Blame Skyrim and my life is over."

Walking out of his office, I have the sudden urge to go home and be with my family. Maybe it's because of what the captain shared with me. Maybe it's the pressure getting to me, but I swear Chase's hugs cure whatever ails me. Frankie, the world would stop spinning without her. I need to go home and appreciate the life I do have.

Chapter Twelve

I thought this was over and done with, but then Logan calls demanding I come down to the lab. Here I sit, with my second cup of coffee, waiting on Logan. He pulls Will into the conversation this time. I caught him driving Miranda's minivan to work. He looks beyond tired, but the DA told us Brandt was still alive in isolation. We're both happy.

"Minivan, huh?"

"Miranda blocked my car in."

"Couldn't move them around?"

"I was tired."

"Uh-huh."

"Fine, she needed my truck to help move a friend. I thought I was off today. Didn't think I'd be sitting here with you and the lollipop guild."

"Wow, the lollipop guild? You just aged yourself, man."

"You knew what I was talking about."

I go to respond, but he's right. I do know who he's referring to. Well, shit. Logan rushes in like a hamster on a few too many espressos. He drops Brandt's laptop on his desk. Then drops his bag on the floor. He sits down, pulls out a bottle of water, and lets out a deep sigh.

"You okay, Logan?"

"Yup, just one too many espresso energy drinks. I had no idea they actually made those kinds of things. Once you have one, they taste so good you end up having like four or five. Before you know it, it's five in the morning, but you totally uncover some great stuff."

"Logan." Will holds up his hand. "It's a bit too early on my day off. Mind explaining to me why we're here? Slowly?"

Logan animatedly takes a few breaths before calming down.

"The laptop is a bust, sort of."

"You couldn't crack it?" I ask flatly. I had hoped to find more information on Garrison in the depths of the hard drive.

"Not all of it, but what I did manage to do might help us."

"Do what?" Will looks exhausted, and this conversation is hard for the two of us with little patience.

"Catch Kiernan Jones."

That gets our attention. We assumed she would pop up eventually and that would be our chance to grab her. There was nothing else to go on.

"Her apartment was cleaned out. Wherever she went, she's off the grid. So, how are you going to find her?"

"She's coming to me."

"Come again?" I ask.

He turns the laptop around to show us a tree of email correspondence. I wish I could understand half of what is in them, but I assume it must be juicy.

"Exchanging porn," I say and Will stifles his laughter. Logan looks confused for a moment before shaking his head.

"No, detective, I bought drugs from her. She posted on various dark websites that she has a surplus of inventory she needed to move right away. Her price undercut a lot of sellers. She's meeting me at the subway station at Forty-Second and Seventh, by the one, two, three lines in six hours."

"How the hell can we corner her in the busiest subway station during rush hour?" Will asks me.

Logan looks lost, but I don't think he had a choice of meeting places.

"We flood the station with plainclothes officers. Make sure the majority of the people on the platform are ours. We use the new cameras to maintain visual and pray like hell. Is she expecting you, Logan, or did you give her fake information?"

His face falls, and I understand that his energy drinks knocked him a bit off his game. He gave her his real name; that might haunt him in the future.

"Does she know anything else about you?"

"No, just I'm a geek in college needing a fix."

"Okay," Will speaks up. "We flood the station, keep tabs on Logan here, and somehow make sure we bring Kiernan in. Piece of cake."

"Exactly."

Somehow, when the captain told me to go home and relax, this was not what I was thinking. Maybe when this is all over. Maybe.

***

Have you ever watched ants in their home? They climb all through the tunnels. Even though they have a distinct order, they walk all over each other, some trying to get out, some trying to get in. Some might just be looking for the queen for some nookie. I don't have a clue. But standing here in the middle of this subway station, I feel like one of those ants.

"Steele, you have eyes on the subject yet?"

"Negative."

She hasn't shown up yet. I don't blame her. She might be turning tail and running. I would. My bigger concern is that she did some digging into Logan and found out who he really is.

One of the officer's voices rings in my ear. "She's on her way down, northernmost staircase."

I turn my attention to Logan. If something happens to him, Hadley would have my head. My job is to keep him safe, one hundred percent. She passes me and walks right up to Logan. She's not wasting any time, but he's slowing her down.

She's desperate, looking around frantically. Each time I lower my hair to block my face. Logan keeps digging through his pockets, looking for more cash. He's good at this acting stuff. Maybe he should make a film with Hadley. No, maybe not; that sounded better in my head.

"Hurry up!" I hear Kiernan say to Logan.

"I'm trying to get it out of my pocket. It's a lot of money. My mom told me not to keep it all in one place," he replies.

I look past them and see Will and the others in position on the opposite end of the platform. The plan is simple. Will gets her attention; she turns and runs into me. I grab her arm, handcuff her, and lead her out of the subway. It's an easy arrest. In theory.

"You know what? Just give me what you have. I can't stay here much longer."

"Okay."

"Have a great high."

She turns and sees Will, and just like we hoped, she turns and runs into me. What I hadn't anticipated was the surge of people pushing me so I lose my grip on Kiernan. She grabs Logan by the sleeve and moves through the crowd. This is not going to end well.

"She's on the move, back up the north side. Crowds causing issues. She's got Pevy. I repeat, the suspect has a hostage."

I push back against the crowd, fighting my way to get closer to her. I can hear the train coming on the express track. It's about a minute or two away. That's going to make it difficult to hear anyone or call for help. Once I break free of the horde, I'm five, maybe six steps behind her when a man pushes her hard. Logan and Kiernan fall onto the train platform. I rush to the side, but the same man pulls me back.

The trains brakes squeal loudly, hurting the ears of all those down here. Too late. My screams blend with the metal hitting metal. I failed Logan. I elbow the man behind me in the gut. He lets go and rushes to the exit. I turn my attention and growing rage back to the male running through the crowd looking for an escape.

"Steele, in pursuit of suspect!"

I run as hard as I can, pushing and shoving my way up the stairs. He jumps the turnstiles and runs up the stairs to the street. I'm only a few steps behind him, darting up the corner, gasping for real air. I rush into Times Square and spin around frantically. Whoever he is, he's gone.

Will follows a few steps behind me, barely out of breath.

"Where'd he go?"

"I have no fucking clue." On an island of thirteen million people, he can hide in plain sight.

Captain Tyler's voice crackles in my ear. "Steele, Everts, report."

"We lost him." I answer. "Logan?"

"Little shit hid with the rats under the platform. We got him out on the other side. Captain's sending him to the hospital for a checkup. He told me to not tell Hadley anything."

"Kiernan?"

"Victor's on his way down."

"Whoever did this, they were following her. Waiting for the right time to strike."

"You're talking a calculated murder. You think Garrison . . ."

"No, cap. I was actually thinking when you are in a desperate situation you have a tendency to do stupid things. She was undercutting other dealers to get rid of her stash. She made more enemies in a few minutes than Garrison probably has in his lifetime. Not that this doesn't help him."

"If she was connected, she can no longer deal. Case closed." Tyler ends the conversation.

The case is closed. The only player left is standing trial. The rest are all dust in the wind.

It's been almost six months, and the mysterious man in the subway tunnel hasn't turned up on any surveillance. We looked through every scrap of video, utilized every facial recognition software. We tried everything at our disposal. The man was truly a ghost.

Seeing the rows of trailers brings a smile to my face. Hadley finally accepted a role in a new local drama series. It isn't a huge part, but the possibility for future episodes is there. She's finally feeling comfortable enough in her own skin to go back to work. I have to thank Logan for that. He's helped her heal when I couldn't. Sometimes family can fail one another, but he has proven worthy of Hadley's adoration.

I haven't given him the whole "hurt her and I know where to bury you" speech. Frankly, he'd probably have his tech friends hack my phone or something to ensure they find him. Maybe develop an app that traces you when you're in trouble even if the phone is off. I laugh at myself for sounding like I understand the words coming out of my mouth.

"Jazz, you're here." Hadley rushes out of her trailer and wraps me up in a tight hug.

"Sorry I'm late."

"No worries. Logan's been bored out of his mind these last few days with me. You guys can talk about some case or whatever. Oh, maybe he can help you with your cell phone!"

"Ms. Moreno, you're wanted on set."

"Coming." She hugs me again. "I'll be back soon, and we'll all go for lunch."

"Go break a leg, preferably not yours."

She laughs at me before straightening up her wardrobe and walking away, the clicking of her heels on the pavement the only sound. Part of me wants to follow and make sure she's okay. I know she's had fittings and read-throughs, but this is her first shot of the day.

"She's got to do this on her own."

Logan puts his hand on my shoulder, and it's the first time I realize the man is taller than me. His video game shirt giving away his geek side. Sadly, I have the same one.

"I'm worried."

"So am I, but we have to let her do this. One thing I've learned: if she needs help, she'll ask. Come on, I've got a sweet computer setup inside."

"How are you feeling? Any residual pain?"

"Nope, all back to my normal geek self."

Logan heads back to the door of the trailer and I'm torn. My feet want to walk away, but my brain can't seem to catch up. I know it's a selfish thing. I have this need to make up for not being there. I want to make it right, even if she says there's nothing to fix. It's purely selfish. It's more about me than her, and I know it, but you feel what you feel.

"Detective?"

Hadley's doing her thing, and I have to let her be. Regardless of my wants, she has to know she can do it on her own. So, I walk to the trailer and wait for her to come to me.

"Holy crap, I am in the wrong industry!"

The trailer is fully decked out with a huge television, gaming system, small kitchen, eating area, and a bed in the back. Logan sits in the small dining area with his laptop. I calmly slide in across from him.

"You want something to drink?"

"No, I'm good. Had two large coffees on the way over."

"Bathroom's in the back on the right before the bedroom."

"This place is nuts."

"Yup, price of hiring union talent."

Logan stares at his computer screen, frantically clicking away on his keyboard.

"I read about Brandt's trial. Good outcome."

"Life without parole works for me. If he lives the entire sentence."

"Yes, there is that."

Logan continues to type on his computer, but his body language is off.

"Got something to tell me?"

"Good and bad. Which do you want first?"

"Hit me with negative first."

"Irving Garrison has been tightening the ranks. He's been doing a better job of hiding his money trails. He's worse than Madoff."

"Even the Teflon Don Gotti slipped up and was convicted. He'll make a mistake. What's the positive?"

"I think we can sort of flush him out with what we have."

"Consider my interest piqued. How is this possible?"

"We release the information we have to the dark web outlets and let them take it from there. There's no guarantee it would go viral, but with his connections to Brandt, Jones, his son's illegal activities, and the truth about your case, as well as what little we can trace to his financial holdings, it just might."

"But this is all sensitive material; releasing it could cost you."

"It's very gray, all circumstantial stuff that you can easily find on the internet if you search for it. I'm just releasing it all in one spot as one unit. Gives it a little more credibility and strength. Might work, might not. It's worth a shot."

"I don't want to risk your career."

"Who's risking anything? If we do this, it will bounce around the world when it uploads from an untraceable, nonexistent IP address. I'm a bit reckless in gaming, not in real life. If anyone tries to track me, it would take weeks or months."

"I will take your word for it as I have no clue what you just said. I will simply trust your judgment."

He smiles, nods, and cracks his knuckles. Before I can say another word, he is frantically typing away like a mad genius. I'm very thankful he's on my team, but I now know and understand a version of Logan works for the enemy. My entire life of training, studying, understanding, and manipulating has to change now. It's all impersonal with emoticons and text messages. The playing field has changed and, as a good general, I need the best warriors. I just pray that the battles ahead don't make me regret my decisions of today.

THE END

About Author

Kimberly Amato is the author of the Jasmine Steele Mystery Series and Enemy. Having won awards for a TV Pilot she co-wrote & produced, she dove headfirst into writing novels. Always creating, jotting down new ideas & unafraid to try new genres, Kimberly writes mysteries, crime, romance, sci-fi & more. Beyond that, she's a podcaster with her wife, Sheila, for the show Forever Fangirls reviewing TV and film on streaming services and in theaters. Kimberly enjoys keeping in touch with her readers. You can find her by using the links below or going to her website KimberlyAmato.com.

amazon.com/stores/Kimberly-Amato/author/B00RKJDIXA

bookbub.com/authors/kimberly-amato

facebook.com/thekimberlyamato

instagram.com/kimberlyamato

Go to the link below to stay up to date on new releases and more!
https://www.kimberlyamato.com/newsletter

Also By Kimberly Amato

THE STEELE SERIES

Steele Intent (Book 1)

Melting Steele (Book 2)

Breaking Steele (Book 3)

Cold Steele (Book 4)

Steele Shield (Book 5)

Steele Influence (Book 6)

STANDALONES

Enemy

www.ingramcontent.com/pod-product-compliance
Lightning Source LLC
Chambersburg PA
CBHW050825180626
46814CB00004B/1461